The Old Sleeper

Other Books by Tom Moates:

The Honest Horsemanship Series

A Horse's Thought
Between the Reins
Further Along the Trail
Going Somewhere
Passing It On

Discovering Natural Horsemanship
Round-Up: A Gathering of Equine Writings
Six Colts, Two Weeks, Volume One
Six Colts, Two Weeks, Volume Two
Considering Horsemanship
The Christian Horseman's Companion

The Old Sleeper

Tom Moates

SPINNING SEVENS
PRESS

SPINNING SEVENS
P R E S S

Cover design by Chris Legg.
ISBN: 978-0-9992465-4-2

Back cover photo by Ken Moates.

Chapter 1

Air Traffic Control Tower
Dulles International Airport
Northern Virginia
1:14 a.m.

"Unidentified aircraft in position 38, 77 traveling 030 at 380 knots, you are approaching restricted airspace for the National Capitol region on an unapproved flight path. Divert course immediately and respond."

Silence.

"Unidentified aircraft traveling 030, squawk 1200.... Identify yourself. You have now entered restricted National Capital airspace. Divert course immediately and respond."

"Mac, I've got a weird one and he's crossed the line," the air traffic controller called to his supervisor across the room.

"No squawk?"

"No squawk signal; no radio contact. He's coming in perfectly straight on a line to Reagan eight miles south of us. He's about over Centreville now. He's pretty much following I-66."

"Great, another wayward Cessna? How many this year already...four?"

"Maybe, but he's cruising...380 knots. And, it's in the middle of the night."

"Okay, I'm on it. I'll call it in to the FAA and the National Capital Region Coordination Center."

"Unidentified aircraft traveling 030, squawk 1200.... Ident. Repeat, you have now entered restricted National Capital airspace. Divert course immediately and respond."

"Mac, I got a bad feeling about this one. It's a bogey. Straight as an arrow, 380 knots steady, and heading right for the heart of D.C."

"NORAD is scrambling two F-16s from Andrews. You should pick them up in a few minutes."

"Yeah, a few minutes. They better hightail it 'cause that's all they've got, if that."

"If they can get off the ground over there, at 25 miles a minute they should intercept him before he's over D.C."

Both men stared silently at the controller's screen. Each moment tick, tick, ticked slowly by..., Nothing. Nothing. Finally, two military aircraft appeared on the screen in Maryland. They exhaled in unison as they watched the F-16s zoom on a course to intercept the steady blip still making a beeline east.

Chapter 2

A Remote Site
West Virginia
6:34 p.m.
The Day Before

The sun dipped below a ridge to the west. In an instant, it ignited a spectacular display of fiery crimson among wispy clouds that seemed to stretch on forever from his vantage point above the tree line. Finally, after climbing through dense forest all afternoon, he reached his destination and was rewarded by the surreal scarlet glow in the heavens.

The sunset faded as quickly as it began. Within minutes, dusk loomed heavy, and he set about gaining his bearings. He walked around the area slowly, looking. Enough light remained to make out parallel metal tracks that ran 30 feet along the ground of a level shelf that jutted out as a natural platform in the mountain side. The metal rails seemed to disappear into the face of a cliff just as he remembered. Up close, a large metal double door became visible recessed a few feet into the rock face. The rails ran straight to the base of the doorway.

The old man, a bit shaky, huffed to catch his breath. The long hours of slow climbing had taken their toll on him; his breathing never was good these days, anyway. Still, he managed a sigh of relief when he saw that the doors remained intact and closed after such long a time.

The old timer produced a small flashlight with a strap from

a jacket pocket which he put around his head. He flipped the light onto high-beam, leaned against the door for a moment, then took a large odd-looking metal key from the other jacket pocket. Click, click...the tumblers in the lock turned as smoothly as they had 64 years ago. The abandoned mine had been easily outfitted for their needs back then. Both large metal doors swung outwards and stood open to reveal a shallow cave. The small beam from his forehead penetrated the darkness and illuminated the biggest secret of his life...one he had given up on, but now finally, incredibly, it was time.

The procedure was straightforward and set up for a single person to execute, and his training came back as a vivid memory from his more youthful days. Everything he needed was there in the decades of dust and in a backpack and plastic gas can he'd packed along, but would it work?

One task after another went like clockwork. As he worked, he thought about how miners had struggled to create the shafts below each wearing a head lamp as he now did, but for very different tasks. Finally, it was time.

He released the brake on the flat car, went around outside, and using a hand winch set up for the job, began cranking. The rig was heavy but well balanced and the sound of the metal wheels screeching along the rusty track got the adrenaline pumping through his old heart.

The car finally came to rest against stops at the end of the rails outside. He reset the brake. Next he cranked a handle on the mobile platform, raising one end of the long metal track attached to it. Fully elevated, he placed a pin in the metal tubing that had telescoped to lock it in place.

The portable control panel looked like a small suitcase from the 1940s with a few switches and buttons. Heavy breathing from the exertion sent him into a violent coughing fit forcing him to stop and hack up phlegm for a few minutes. When it finally subsided and he could breathe again, he grabbed the control panel and a reel of wire and let the wire unspool as he walked down hill with it and set up behind a boulder for safety.

Everything was ready.

A glance at his watch revealed it was nearly 1:00 a.m. He was surprised so many hours had passed, but the activity of the tasks at hand had made time fly. Just as he had dreamed of doing a thousand times, he turned a switch on the bottom left corner of the panel, then followed that by pushing a button on the right. It fired up and began to roar on idle setting at the bottom of the long rail. With a huge sigh of relief, he clapped and then rubbed his hands together like a mad scientist in some old movie.

"Ah, Bertha...may you find your mark!" he croaked aloud, thrilled at his mission's near success.

Without further hesitation, he flipped another switch, pressed two buttons simultaneously, looked up at the fiery glow illuminating the rock face of the mountainside, then released them.

There was an explosive whooshing as the pulse jet engine went to full throttle and the booster rocket ignited. In its fury, the yellow glow of a five foot flame lit the scene around him like an artificial sun. The heat from it warmed his face, even at his considerable distance from the launching area.

He became dismayed, watching as the roaring fire just sat there with its deafening buzz...three seconds, four seconds, five seconds.... "Is something wrong; did I forget something?" he wondered.

But then, the holding pin sheared and the long-hidden secret hurled 350 feet per second eastward, flying. He sat in awe as the violent chopping noise faded and the massive flame in the sky diminished from a huge plume to a tiny spec. Then, it was gone.

Chapter 3

George Mason University
Fairfax, Virginia
1:16 a.m.

"You've got to see my new tires," Dave said. "31.10-50s...they look awesome on the truck. I'm ready for some serious rootin' now!"

"Sure, let's go have a look," Ed replied.

The two students stepped out into the parking lot of the Patriot Center, a 10,000 seat arena at George Mason University in Fairfax, Virginia. They both worked part time as overnight security guards at the arena and Ed had just arrived a few minutes late to take a shift over from Dave.

"What's that weird sound? Do you hear that?" Ed asked.

"Yeah, that crazy buzzing? It's getting louder. Sounds like something is chopping the air. A helicopter, maybe?"

The sophomores looked up to the west in time to see a flash of fire streak across right overhead about 1000 feet in the air. The noise it made was like some demonic combination of a huge propeller aircraft and a semi passing on the highway. It was unlike anything they had heard before or seen in a night sky.

"Dude!" Dave managed to blurt out and, holding his cell phone in his hands since he had been texting and walking, with a couple of swift thumb motions he was filming the aerial phenomenon.

"It's a UFO!" Ed shrieked, his voice raising an octave and barely audible over the droning coming from the aircraft. In 25 seconds, it was out of sight to the east, but the buzzing, chopping sound was audible in the distance for some time before it faded, too.

"I got it on video—look!"

Dave and Ed huddled together and watched the screen on the phone. The video was shaky but caught several good moments showing the plume of fire streaming behind some dark object as it flew through the air overhead. The audio gave them both a shiver as the distinctive droning, buzzing sound replayed.

Chapter 4

Arlington, Virginia
1:18 a.m.

"This is Stroke One, I have a visual—there's a good sized fire plume behind that thing."

"Lock target, Stroke One, and standby. Stroke Two, can you see what it is? Is it a plane?"

"No, I can't see the aircraft, only a huge fire plume coming from a jet engine, I'd say. No wait...it just went dark. I could see the flame behind the aircraft a second ago but it just went dark."

"Stroke One, you are cleared to engage, repeat...you are cleared...."

The F-16 pilots saw a massive explosion ahead of them. 15 seconds later they whizzed by it. They quickly circled back and flew low to get a better look.

"It exploded! Holy smokes that thing is huge! It must have been a missile, guys. There's a massive fireball on the ground and a ton of smoke going skyward. It detonated on the Virginia side of the river. I can see it's between the Pentagon and Reagan. What do you see, Stroke Two?"

"Guys, it hit the highway. That mess of 395—all that cloverleaf just before the bridge across the Potomac—it looks like it's been blasted. It's a mess."

"Stay there and cover the area, Stroke One and Two. We're

scrambling more fighters to cover the no fly zone and shutting down all air traffic. Maintain a close orbit over the area until further notice."

Chapter 5

Incident Site
Arlington, Virginia
3:12 a.m.

The tractor trailer was waved through the police barricade and parked just fifteen feet back from the edge where the pavement ended in a jagged crater. An hour before, that point had been in the middle of Interstate 395 right at a tangled web of roads and clover leafs where 395 intersected with routes 1 and 110 just before crossing the Potomac. Now, the interchanges were a series of highways that abruptly fell off into a massive crater of twisted rebar, concrete, and pavement illuminated by the ghoulish glow of fires across the area.

Two men hopped out of the front of the rig and looked around. They stood at the edge of the precipice and gazed at the destruction. A few fire trucks were managing to get their streams of water onto the flames, but the center of the blast zone was beyond their reach. Just below them, they could see a car that must have driven off the edge of the Interstate just after the blast. It stood nose down in the rubble. A team of firefighters were working around it to get somebody out.

"What a mess," said the Officer in Charge, Lieutenant Schmitt, in a shaky voice as much to himself as to the man beside him.

Master Chief, Rick McAbee, just uttered a guttural, "Humph," turned on his heel and headed for the door to the trailer. With two steady strides he was inside the state of the art Explosive Ordinance Disposal mobile base unit. The three junior crewmen had been busy at work already and had the stairs in place, communications on line, and now were hovering over an array of computers.

"Three million dollars worth of stuff in here, boys, and what's the most important piece of equipment?" he shot at them.

"The coffee pot, Master Chief!" the Petty Officers replied in unison, not looking up from their tasks.

McAbee found his plastic, United States Navy thermal mug in a cabinet, filled it with black coffee that already sat on a counter freshly brewed in the coffee maker, and took a sip. He walked around to check on the men's activities. Each was busy with his pre-assigned task and the Explosive Ordinance Disposal mobile base was up and running.

"Petty Officer Jackson, what's your assessment? Tell me what we aren't dealing with," McAbee said.

"The good news is we're not picking up any Weapons of Mass Destruction, Master Chief. It seems to have been a conventional munition."

"Right. Jackson, stay with the base. Davies and Howard, you two get geared up and we'll start working on the site forensics ASAP. Let's figure out what this thing was before the country wakes up and all hell breaks loose."

Chapter 6

Casa Del Sol Care Community
Wickenburg, Arizona
The Previous Day

"Mr. Levin, you've got a guest!" the nurse chimed in her happy manner that made the old man roll his eyes and cringe as she glided through the open doorway into the small room and exited just as quickly.

Vassily lay in bed watching the news on a television that was mounted towards the top of the opposite wall. He hit the mute and wondered who could possibly be there to see him. He had never had a visitor. His days now were mostly monotonous. At 82 with no family remaining, his beloved Katerina gone, and some "health issues," as he liked to refer to the cancer that recently had returned from a 15 year remission, this was highly irregular.

Bob Jones popped his balding head around the corner.

"Heya Vassily," he said with his thick Georgia accent. "How they treating you up here?"

When Bob brought the rest of himself into the doorway, he looked like a manikin from an Old Navy commercial, Vassily thought, wearing frumpy cargo pants, a flannel shirt, an unzipped hooded sweatshirt, and those funny boating shoes without socks. Attire that screamed "casual" was one of Vassily's pet peeves about the American culture—oh how they enjoyed basking in underachievement, disrespect, and lack of discipline—but he had spent the latter half of his life keeping such thoughts close to his chest.

"Bob! Vrell, vrut a surprise," Vassily said with his still fairly thick Russian accent, faking a smile. "How's zee place? I hope you know I zold you zat house az-iz last year...no vrarranties if zee microwave fried!"

"Aw shoot naw," the forty-something fellow shot back at him. "The place is great! Kathy and I love it."

Bob came into the room and stood at the edge of the bed. Vassily held out a hand and gave the younger man a firm handshake.

"This came for you," Bob said, pulling an envelope from his back pocket and handing it to Vassily.

A couple decades had passed since Vassily had run across a once common place pale blue envelope with alternating red and dark blue slanted tabs framing the periphery. This one had a set of wings left of the address, below which read: "Par Avion, By Airmail, Mit Luftpost." His pulse shot up.

"Vrell, vrell...zanks for dropping zat by," Vassily said.

He took the envelope and quickly looked it over before setting it as nonchalantly as he could manage on a table on the side of the bed opposite Bob beside an untouched tray of oatmeal and green Jell-O.

"I thought it was a tad odd since all your other mail has been forwarded since you moved. I figured being airmail and all it might be important and I'd better just drop it on by. Got any idea who it's from?"

"Yah," Vassily said, and cleared his throat. "No return address...but I uzed to get junk mail like zis all zee time from traveling overseas on business—I'm zure zat's all it is. Zorry you came all zee vray across town for zat, Bob. My address forwarding order must have expired at zee post office. I'm afraid you might be zeeing more of zis junk in your mailbox."

"Aw shoot," Bob again used one of his habitual phrases, "no problem, Vassily. If more comes I'll collect it and drop it by again sometime. I work over this way once in awhile. Glad to see you're doing okay."

Vassily managed more chitchat with the acquaintance who had purchased his house. Even though Bob's visit was a pleasant change to his mostly lonely existence, he got rid of him by saying he wasn't feeling very well and was going to take a nap. The instant the younger man exited the room Vassily sat bolt upright and grabbed the envelope. He studied it closely, flipping it over front to back several times. The postmark was from London, his name and old address was printed on a label and stuck on the front.

"Could it possibly be?" Vassily whispered aloud. "Could zis really be it after all zese years, Katerina?"

He gazed upon the photo of the woman with shoulder length brunette hair that sat on a dresser below the TV. She had been twenty-two when the photo had been taken, and they were about to be married in Moscow while they both were on leave from the military.

Another photo sat beside the first one from the same time period. Vassily looked at the photo of him, young, strong, on top of the world, a serious look on his face, standing in his flying gear beside a Yak-9 prop fighter. He had shown such promise flying the older Yak-9s left over from World War II in his early pilot training that a few months later he was chosen to attend the Armavir Higher Military Aviation School for Pilots, 850 miles straight south of Moscow to begin his jet fighter training.

Thinking about that time in his life before The Mission, as he and Katerina had called it, was both joyful and painful. Mostly, he tried to block it from his mind these days to keep from feeling bitter all the time.

"How long vre vraited together to get zee vrord, always ready to be able to do our part again, yes...once more! But instead, vratched our dreams die zee slowest of deaths. But now, I've got a feeling zis is it, Katinka! I can feel it."

Vassily took an old, worn pocket knife from the table, opened a small blade, and carefully cut open the top of the fine, light paper envelope. He removed a single sheet of paper and unfolded it. The paper had a logo from a British travel agency at the top and the letter read:

> Dear Mr. Levin,
>
> Congratulations! You have won an all expense paid trip to Greece!
>
> Please call our offices between October 9 and October 11 for details between the hours of 9:00 a.m. and 4:00 p.m. Your winner's authentication number is: 6949.
>
> Have a wonderful day!

The old man began to shake and tears filled his eyes. It was here! Finally, it was here.

Chapter 7

EOD Mobile Command Center
Arlington, Virginia
5:32 a.m.

"Master Chief, what are you saying?" Officer in Charge
Schmitt asked, cocking his head sideways with a stupefied look on
his face.

"You really need me to repeat all that, Sir?"

"Yes, Master Chief McAbee...I do," he replied. "Here
I've been thinking the most likely scenario is a Cessna full of
explosives trying for a kamikaze on the Pentagon right over there,
or maybe a SCUD missile. Either way, definitely the work of
organized and funded terrorists to be able to attack us from our
own back yard, so, I'm really not sure I heard you right. Give me
those facts again, and keep in mind I have to brief the Secretary
of Defense in five minutes and he's hammering me to give him
something definitive for the White House to provide the public at
a press conference live on TV at 11:00 a.m."

The two men again were standing where they had begun this
job a few hours earlier, in the middle of what normally would
have been a lane of 395 traffic. At the moment, however, it was
a shelf of concrete between the Explosive Ordinance Disposal
mobile command unit and the jagged torn edge of pavement
where the Interstate simply ended at a drop-off that disappeared

into the twisted mess of the blast zone.

Dawn was breaking to the east and the soft glow of daylight revealed a thick plume of smoke rising out of the crater into the air. It wafted east towards the Capitol.

A dozen other trucks and vans were inside the police barricade now, and the traffic lanes and shoulders of that stretch of 395 instead of showing a typical flow of traffic on the increase for rush hour served as a parking lot. Vehicles of all kinds were crammed around the EOD truck. Everybody seemed to be on-site—FBI, Homeland Security, Department of Defense Military Police, the local EMS and Fire Departments—and each entity had a command center set up in this secured area.

Sirens wailed constantly in the distance audible over the monotonous droning of generators which hummed all around them. Just outside the police barricade at least a dozen microwave link poles were visible, raised into the air from TV news crew vans.

The bottleneck of the whole operation at this moment rested on the shoulders of the EOD crew. With no detection of chemical, biological, or radiological agents from the start, rescue crews had been given the green light to charge in and get to work. Everywhere they were digging through the wreckage looking for injured people, and fire crews were fighting to contain the blazes still burning here and there.

It was clear now that the whole area was a crime scene caused by a terrorist attack on the United States capital and any evidence in the blast zone needed to be carefully documented and analyzed. Answers needed to be found and the culprits brought to justice. It also was going to be a big mess to balance between a critical rescue operation and the gathering of forensic evidence to answer the big questions, and fast. But the EOD team had made progress.

"It's like this, Sir," Master Chief McAbee said, making a karate chop with his right hand onto the palm of his left to try and center the young Lieutenant's focus a little more this time. "Our guys recovered part of a wooden wing and a large metal tube so far, among other smaller pieces from the weapon. It may be hard to believe, but I know what we're looking at here. When we get all the pieces together and analyzed, you're going to find this is an FZG-76."

"An FZG-76?" OIC Schmitt repeated cluelessly.

"The metal tube is part of an Argus pulse jet engine which propelled it. The wooden wing absolutely fits the model. And in an amazing stroke of luck, the nose cone was recovered because a fire fighter found it and thought the odd thing might be part of the weapon and called us in to have a look. It's a definitive clue because it has an odometer driven by a vane anemometer, so it's got to be one...or clearly a knock off of one."

"A what?"

"Uh, right...a little prop turns on the nose cone of the rocket as it speeds through the air which counts the mileage and when it has traveled the desired distance to the target, it kills the fuel so the pulse jet quits and it dives to earth and detonates on impact. How it survived, I'll never know. A total fluke.

"And look at the blast zone," McAbee gestured with a sweep of his right arm out across the smoldering mess from their vantage point. "600 yards from the center of where it hit and detonated in every direction is completely pulverized, and I bet the shock wave busted every windshield in the parking lots on this side of the Pentagon over there—which is consistent with a blast made by one ton of high explosives detonated on impact with the ground, which is exactly what we'd expect from one of those rockets."

"Okay, so one more time, Master Chief," the OIC rubbed his temples with his fingers. "In English, what is this thing?"

"What we have here, sir, is a genuine FZG-76...you know,

a German V-1 rocket...a buzz bomb, a doodlebug. In a way it's brilliant. We know from the incoming radar reports that they launched it from a rural area to the west, probably West Virginia...even if that thing was sitting stationary for years in some forgotten bunker or even just a barn on some old farm in the mountains, it could work fine. These things fly on your basic low octane regular unleaded gas. The only other things necessary to fly it would be a small air compressor to charge the onboard tanks pre-flight and a small battery to ignite the fuel mix which is done with a simple spark plug—and they'd need some type of launch rail pointed east. The rocket has a crude guidance system that would put it on the general course to its target once it's flying.

"The Germans catapulted these rockets into flight with a steam piston deal, and then the pulse jet engine propelled the rocket during flight. But, if this one had a solid fuel setup for that launching stage of the operation—you know, basically like our Tomahawks—it could have been setting somewhere since the 40s and literally, fill it up with regular, check the air in the pressure tanks, hook up the battery, and here we are."

"Master Chief," the OIC said, not looking any less deer-in-the-headlights than before, "you're saying that I'm supposed to tell the Sec Def that a Nazi buzz bomb from the 40s just nearly hit the Pentagon?"

"That would be accurate, sir."

There was a long silence. McAbee stood and watched the Lieutenant rub his temples again.

"Okay then..." the OIC finally said. "This'll be fun. I've gotta life sized picture of how this call is going to go. You come straight to me with anything else you find, especially if you have even a hint of something more...more...plausible."

"It was before my time, sir, but if it helps, the guys I worked with in my early days said that in the early 50s they all used to work on V-1s that we brought back from Germany after World War II for cruise missile training. There were quite a few of these things around. And we need to keep in mind that the old Allied nations took the German models after the war and toyed with their own versions for awhile. I never expected to see something like this, but I'm just giving you the facts. We'll keep on it and before long I'll have more to go on."

The OIC walked off shaking his head to make his call to the Secretary of Defense from a secure video link in the truck.

"You've gotta be fricking kidding me..." McAbee heard the Lieutenant say to himself as he walked away.

Chapter 8

Lazy G Ranch
Near Salome, Arizona
7:15 a.m.

75 degrees and sunny, it was a perfect October morning. The Quarter Horse was a tall, big boned, ranch type—a sorrel with a blaze and socks in the rear. Gene enjoyed the feeling between them as the gelding reached with each step, walking out with a purpose as they headed towards a small bunch of cattle in some mesquite across a wash in the distance.

Ring. Ring. Gene's cell phone made the bell-ringing sound of an old time telephone. That ring tone, the default setting by choice, reminded him of a pleasant past where a telephone was just a telephone and nothing more. And, even though the flip phone he doggedly refused to part with was nearly an antique now in the world of smart phones, that ringing brought back memories of the hard, heavy hand-piece of the black telephone that connected by a cord to the base with its rotary dial that used to be in his grandparents' ranch house when he was a kid. That ringing brought back to him a time when things were solid, lasted, and usually got passed down from one generation to the next.

Continuing on at a brisk walk between two particularly old saguaro cacti that towered above Dusty and him, he drew the

phone from the holster on the belt of his shotgun chaps and
deftly flipped it open with the thumb on the same hand.

"I see 'em," he blurted out, not giving the caller the chance
for a first word in. "I'll get them back towards that other bunch
directly, probably take an hour I reckon."

"Nice to talk to you too, Gene."

"Aw naw...I'm on my first week of real retirement here Jeb...
the *first week*. I'm 68 years old and surely you can shuffle all those
papers without the help of a washed up old field guy like me."

"Gene, I gotta ask you a few things. It's important. Real
important."

"Right. You got five minutes which is how long it'll take me
and Dusty here to get to the far side of these cow/calf pairs and
head back towards the rodear."

"What the heck...no, never mind, I don't even want to know
what that means, cowboy. Look, you haven't seen the news have
you, Gene?"

"Jeb, my goal in life is to never watch the news again, and I'm
off to a pretty good start except for you intruding on my works
here today."

"We gotta talk...it can't be over the phone and it can't wait.
I'll fly out to you. I'll be at that little airstrip by your place this
afternoon."

"I'll be back at the place by dark, but we'll be branding the
rest of the week so make it quick, will ya. I've got a really early
morning."

"Fair enough. Get on little doogies."

"Jeb, you're an idiot."

"Good thing you're retired or I could have you up for
insubordination on that one."

"Oh, there's plenty more where that came from. I've been
storing them up for decades, Maestro."

"Right, right...you know we only let you retire so you

wouldn't infect these youngsters coming along with your pitiful attitude."

"Time's up, *Jefe*! Got cows to gather."

The phone clacked shut, and with a swift motion it was back in its holster. Gene and Dusty gently circled the small mob of mostly black baldies and with a little coaxing the cattle began moving slowly towards the south.

Chapter 9

Casa Del Sol Care Community
Wickenburg, Arizona
The Previous Afternoon

Vassily began planning right away. He would need a rental car. He would probably need a stash of pain killers to curb the worst of his pain if it got bad. October 10th was tomorrow, so there was a little time to plan but no time to waste. He couldn't remember the last time he felt this way—excited, important, remembered. Everything Vassily had secretly stood for in his life while living in America suddenly rushed back and he felt incredibly young again.

The old man did his best to keep up his crabby persona and not show any changes to the nurses and other residents that day. He was feeling better—actually physically better than he had in months—perhaps an affect of the great news, but he complained all the more to the staff about his pains and made a small cache of the pain medications they brought to him.

He already knew every detail of the staff's regular comings-and-goings. It was a slack affair, after all, not many assisted-living patients are quick movers or trying to get away to somewhere else. It wasn't a break out anyway; he was paying to be there, paying a lot, and should in theory be free to go whenever he wanted, but he needed to be sure not to raise suspicions.

Vassily knew it was terminal this time. The doctors remained optimistic when they visited him but he knew better. He was guessing he had a few months, tops. But with the simple opening of a letter, he had regained purpose—his big purpose, his life's purpose—which he thought had passed by him long ago. Every time he thought about the letter he gloried at the opportunity to achieve his mission, finally!

On the bright side, the cancer situation meant his own safety wasn't a huge factor in his plans. He had always been prepared to readily give his life for his country at any point along the way, so it was particularly liberating. If only Katerina were there to help as they'd planned together, but then again, being a lone wolf might be best.

Chapter 10

James S. Brady Press Briefing Room
The White House
Washington, D.C.
11:00 a.m.

"At 1:20 a.m. this morning the United States was attacked,"
the President said from behind his podium, the oval White House
emblem hanging behind his head, an American flag draped
around a pole to his right, and the Presidential flag likewise to his
left.

"America awakened to the news this morning that an
explosion occurred near the Pentagon. A single deliberate and
deadly attack has been carried out against us and the victims
of it were innocent, unsuspecting motorists—men, women,
and children. Preliminary reports indicate that the blast was
caused by a missile armed with conventional explosives. We
have confirmed there are no radioactive, biological, or chemical
weapons associated with this explosion. The missile impacted a
section of Interstate 395 and other roads in the area between the
Pentagon and Reagan National Airport. No one has yet claimed
responsibility for this cowardly act of terrorism against our citizens
and our Capital.

"There is no evidence of any other attacks at this time. At this
hour, all air traffic across the United States has been suspended

until further notice and all civilian aircraft are accounted for at present and on the ground.

"Our military experts have been on the scene for hours already working in tandem with police and rescue personnel to provide accurate information about the weapon that has been launched against us. Trust me...we will soon discover who is behind this and they will be brought to justice.

"The U. S. Terror-Alert status has been raised to Red—Severe. All of the resources at our disposal are on full alert but there are no indications of coordinated attacks or heightened chatter among known terrorist organizations at this time.

"Make no mistake, this clearly is an attack on the United States of America—an act of war against us. Terrorists expect that their evil deeds of death and destruction will throw our nation into chaos and confusion. That America will be bullied and will retreat when attacked in so cowardly a fashion. But, America always has and always will fight for the freedoms we enjoy— liberty that is the very foundation of our great nation. No extremists or rouge regime with the desire to crush freedom and impose whatever brand of dictatorship they are selling will *ever* defeat the thriving nation made up of so many great and varied peoples that is the United States of America. We will defend our freedoms and stand up for all that is good and just at home and around the world."

Among a cacophony of camera clicks and reporters futility waving pens and saying, "Mr. President...Mr. President," the President turned away from the familiar faces of the White House press corps and walked briskly out of the room.

Chapter 11

Lazy G Ranch
Near Salome, Arizona
5:34 p.m.

The branding went better than Gene had expected. The cows, a rather motley mix of all kinds he'd picked up here and there, mostly cooperated on the gathering and his help proved to be a solid bunch of cow hands. As the ranch owner, Gene was the boss for the branding. He kept thinking about how many years had passed since he had run a branding crew—they could be counted in decades. The last time had been up in Nevada was after he had returned from Vietnam. He had just gotten out of the Navy and was at a branding on his grandparent's place when the old patriarch had been laid up following a hip replacement.

While he was growing up, Gene's parents' place had been close to the family ranch in Nevada, and Gene had spent all the time he could helping out his grandfather. He would ride a horse several miles over to help work with cattle, fix fences, shoe horses, repair barns, feed...anything that went on about the ranch was fun for him. Every day had been an adventure, and he had felt at home on the land and among the animals.

Gene had learned to brand by gathering cattle in a fence corner or against rim rock in one of the many multi-thousand acre pastures on the place into a group they called a "rodear." The cowboys then roped and worked the cattle in the open out of the rodear. He knew down in this Arizona country it was probably more likely folks brought the cattle to a set of pens, split off the cows and calves, and branded in smaller corrals. He had decided to stick with what he knew, in part because he loved it. The other part of the decision was that the pens on the place he'd bought were in disrepair. Luckily, what his grandfather had taught him and those earlier experiences came back to him. He lined things out with the crew to his liking and everything was going smoothly.

As a relative newcomer to the area, Gene was especially glad that the crew had clicked with him. He knew cattlemen and women tend to be a fiercely independent lot, and while not unfriendly in general, they tended to have little use for someone who strolled into their neighborhood and gave them an uneasy feeling. Distrust didn't take much to germinate sometimes.

On that first day, there had been a fun atmosphere with plenty of razzing between the hands. It had reminded him of being around his grandparents' crew and old times. They had finished up well before dark with the cattle that had been gathered for that day. Gene then had led a line of dusty pickups and stock trailers—horses still saddled and loaded in them—over to his house for the traditional after branding meal.

Gene had recently moved into the ranch house and lived there alone. It was a U shaped structure, with the elbows of the U at right angles. A terracotta tile roof protected the place from the elements. The roof on all three sections overhung the exterior walls on the inside of the U making a partially covered courtyard. The rafters landed on stout beams that rested atop weathered wooden posts, long ago debarked but otherwise in their natural roundness. The posts sat atop short stone columns. The part of the house that comprised the bottom section of the U was one large open room with kitchen, living, and dining space all together. One leg of the U contained his bedroom and office; the one opposite held two guest rooms, all of which had double doors that opened into the courtyard.

The courtyard was Gene's favorite spot. It was nestled within the three sides of the house and the open end looked out over an expanse of desert beyond which he could see mountains rising in the distance. The ranch property bordered on Bureau of Land Management land, so no structures were in sight in that direction, only 30,000 acres of open, dusty high desert. It was the kind of spot he'd always dreamed of retiring to. He could hardly believe that after all those years of holding onto that vision, he now sat at a simple metal table in a matching chair with a nice rocking bounce to it having a glass of water with a dozen of his new acquaintances hanging around and chattering about the day's branding highlights on his own place. It was a dream come true.

Gene had learned long ago that anytime cows, horses, and people interact, you get good stories, and today had been no exception. Even though some of the crew had kept an eye on the big news coming out of Washington, D. C. with their cell phones and the talk circled back to it occasionally, there was no keeping the day's branding stories from getting recounted now that they were relaxing.

A neighbor whom everybody called Pablo—Gene wasn't sure why because he knew his real name was Tim—was explaining about his perfect throw while roping calves. The loop traveled just perfectly for the calf he had aimed at, but the bugger had jumped clear through it before he could take up the slack for a catch...then, the very same thing happened again with the same calf on his next shot.

A tall, skinny fellow with a worn straw cowboy hat, jeans, and an apron with a picture of Yosemite Sam holding two bottles of hot sauce instead of pistols and the words, "Back Off Varmints!" came out through the doorway with a big tray of burgers already on buns. He set them down on a table that was stacked with potato salad, baked beans, chips, salsa, and other delicacies. The hungry cow hands grabbed plates and started filling them up, still laughing at Pablo's plight.

"Glad to hear the day went well," Bruce said as he came over to where Gene was sitting.

"I sure appreciate your taking the position of cook for these few days. Takes a load off my mind."

"You know I appreciate a little work, Gene. And it ain't the first time I've cooked for a rough and rowdy crew of cowpokes."

"I've got to go meet a fellow for a little bit. He's flying in. I thought he might be here already, but since he's not I might just ride down to the airpark and meet up with him there."

"Must be important—him flying in and you putting off supper after a day of branding."

Gene looked at Bruce who had a slight twinkle in his eye and realized the cook, a former Gunnery Sergeant in the Marine Corps, had been keeping up with the news coming out of D.C. all day—including the no-fly lockdown across the country.

"Naw...well...it's my old boss needing something. Really, I think he just couldn't pass up the chance to fly out here and ruin my good spirits on my first week of retirement. And, if you haven't learned this about me yet, Gunny, I'm a sucker for airplanes and he flies some nice birds. Just leave me a couple burgers on the stove, will ya?"

"Sure thing, Boss. Breakfast at 4:30 a.m. I'll be ringing that triangle."

"Sounds good. See ya then."

Chapter 12

Casa Del Sol Care Community
Wickenburg, Arizona
3:30 p.m.

    Vassily showered, shaved, and dressed. He packed his laptop into its case along with the two photos from his dresser and the few pain killers he'd gathered. Each move he made in the process was thoughtful, deliberate, and unhurried. Every little detail in his environment now packed a newfound interest for him—colors, sounds, smells all were incredibly vivid. He had turned off the television during the day for the first time since he'd arrived at the retirement home and he practiced paying attention and mapping everything that was in the environment around him in his mind as he'd been trained to do so many years ago.

    Now, something so mundane as how he wrapped the cord to the power supply for his computer and stowed it in the bag, or placed his cell phone in the breast pocket of his suit coat, held intense interest for him. It was strange, but he felt somehow reborn into his own life. He picked up the pocketknife from the table beside the bed and looked at its worn wooden handle. It had been a gift from a commanding officer to commend his excellent flying half a century ago. He opened both blades and looked at where they were stamped with a small Soviet stars with sickle and hammer insignias superimposed on them. The edges of his mouth curled upwards into a smile—an unusual position for his face these days. The blades clicked as he shut them before he stowed the prized possession in his pants pocket.

Checking around the room for any little item that might give him away thrilled him, although he knew there were none. The only thing related to his mission in the room was that letter from London, and Bob was the only one who knew about it. It was in his shirt pocket under his vest by his heart; he felt for it just to make sure it really was still there. Even if that letter was discovered, there was nothing about its message that could possibly raise an eyebrow or give him or the mission away. The thrill of his life was back and his old comrades finally were making a move.

Vassily wore his best suit. For ease of a quick getaway and to give the impression that he had not pulled up stakes and left, he would leave his other clothes and belongings behind just as they were. He could get what he needed once he was away. He knew the staff wouldn't check on him before dinner time, which gave him several hours head start before his absence would be noticed. He decided to turn the TV on so the room would seem normal and the typical noises would be there in case anyone happened by. When he took the remote from the table by the bed and flipped the TV on.

Vassily figured that when the staff discovered he was missing, most likely they would figure he was puttering around the place somewhere and would make a half hearted search for him at first. Worst case scenario, they would figure he had gone a little senile and wandered off the grounds into the neighborhood, make a quick search around the grounds, and then call the police.

None of that mattered if he could get from his room and out to the street undetected. By the time dinner rolled around and they found he was missing, he would be situated and it wouldn't matter when they discovered his disappearance.

The old Russian was set. He paused for a second to look around one last time. Then he shouldered the laptop bag, went to the door, and peered out. The room entered into a long hallway with windows opposite the rooms which faced the parking lot. No one was in sight. He took a deep breath and set out, closing the door quietly behind him.

The afternoon sun reflected off of car windshields into the hallway. Vassily reached in his suit coat pocket and took out his dark aviator's sunglasses and slipped them on as he walked briskly along. At the end of the hallway, a small tree stood at the corner in a large pot. He paused there for a moment and peered through the branches and leaves into the lobby. There stood his doctor with a couple of the nurses talking. He frowned, thinking about the times in severe pain when he had wished he could have found that scoundrel who was nowhere to be found. He probably had been on the golf course, he thought. "Zeez Americans!" he muttered to himself. And now that he was the last person Vassily needed between him and the door, there he was.

Something welled up inside Vassily then, emboldening him. It wasn't something he thought through. It was, rather, some brash reflex. He straightened up and walked right past the doctor and nurses to the door. He gave a pistol shot with his thumb and pointer finger to the regular clerk who sat behind the front desk as he pushed the door open with the other hand and walked right out into the warm afternoon.

He didn't look back.

If he had, he would have seen that his doctor only paid attention to the nurses, the nurses paid him no attention whatever as he walked by, and the desk clerk had never even looked up at him. It was as if he had been invisible.

He walked across the parking lot and down the block, and he knew that, at least for now, he truly was invisible.

Chapter 13

Harquahala Hills Airpark
Salome, Arizona
5:48 p. m.

The little airpark was just a few miles down a gravel road from the ranch. The close proximity of the airpark to Gene's ranch was no random occurrence. He had spent much of his spare time during the last decade of his career searching the Internet for the perfect place to accommodate both of his obsessions: working with horses and cattle and flying planes.

Gene had first qualified as a pilot while in the Navy back in the 1960s flying A-4s in Test Pilot School, but then the Vietnam War broke out. The highlight of his military career in the Navy had been shooting down two Mig-21s flying an F-4 Phantom over North Vietnam in a single dogfight within three minutes of one another and saving his wingman in the process, a feat which made him rather famous among his peers at the time.

But, it was the old prop planes of the World War II era that truly captivated Gene's imagination. He was an avid student of the dogfight. He spent hours carefully dissecting every maneuver from any accounts he could find, from World War I era planes to the latest jet fighters. When he could manage it, he was thrilled to go up in some restored or replica war bird, from either World War, and fake dog fight with another capable pilot. Those chances were precious few, but he was connected to other such enthusiasts through online forums and clubs which helped line them up sometimes. Love of the World War II fighters was one thing he and his former boss, Jeb, had in common.

Just inside the entrance to the airpark sat a little clubhouse, a few hangers, and a fuel station. Houses and RVs sat back off the runway on lots with yards in front of them—some had palm trees, others cacti, and one had a colorful variety of bird feeders. He pulled up in front of a large hanger with the door half open and got out of the truck.

"Hey, Gene," he heard from inside the hanger.

"Hey there, Conrad," he replied, recognizing the voice. "How you doing, old-timer?"

"Old-timer my foot. Have you looked in the mirror lately, kiddo?"

"Naw, never do. That's how I keep this aura of youthfulness. What-cha working on in here?"

Gene slipped into the hanger and when his eyes adjusted to the darker light he rubbed them hard and then looked again to be sure he wasn't seeing a mirage.

"Jumpin' jeemeny crickets, Conrad! Where on earth did you get this project?"

"Ha-haa!" the old airman crowed. "Wouldn't you like to know!"

"Yes I would! A Sopwith Pup...that's a full scale replica, right? But wait, that's not a...."

"Yep. An original, authentic, honest-to-goodness Le Rhône rotary engine!"

"Holy guacamole, Conrad! Where did you get it? I'm going to have to come by more often."

"It'll be my winter project, but come spring when it's ready I'll let you take it up."

"I'll be here. Heck, I'll come by and hand you tools."

"What brings you by? You know you can't fly out anywhere. All air traffic across the country has been grounded because of the attack in D.C."

"Yeah, I did hear that. Someone on my branding crew had a smart phone and told us about some kind of explosion and gave us a few details. What have you heard?"

"They're saying it was a missile of some sort, not an airplane or a car bomb. Still no real info as far as I'm concerned—that's really all they've reported so far. Of course, all anybody is talking about on the news is what kind of missile jihadists might get their hands on. They're just filling up TV time—blah, blah, blah—non-stop with anything they can jabber on about when they really have nothing new to report. 'Scud' is the new favorite catch-word of the day, and if you need a primer on scuds, just watch five minutes of TV and you'll be up to speed on their makes, models, range, and payload capabilities. Luckily, whatever it was hit the highway and not the Pentagon or Reagan Airport nearby, so very little damage was done considering, and they have very few casualties."

"Well, I'm sure that explains it."

"Explains what?"

"I've got a friend flying in tonight for a quick visit."

"But that's not possible."

Conrad glanced up from what he was doing and caught Gene's eye.

"Oh, I see. It is possible then," the older man said, focusing back at his unbolting.

"Afraid so, Gramps. Would it be alright if he parks here at your place? I'd take him down to my hanger but he's just making a quick in-and-out."

"Sure. What's he flying?"

"I dun-know. I'm guessing a company Cessna Skyhawk, but this guy can surprise you sometimes."

Gene started inspecting the Pup up close. The frame was constructed of steel tubing rather than the original wood framing, but not the aluminum strutting he'd seen on some modern World War I bi-plane replicas.

"A guy up in Kingman built it in 1968 from an original set of plans," Conrad said, still fussing with a bolt on the top wing. "The fabric is sketchy, so I'm going to pull the whole plane apart, go through everything while I'm at it, and refabric the bird. I heard he bought the engine from a guy in France and had it shipped over and rebuilt it himself. Amazing luck!"

"I'll sure take it up for you when it's ready. You just let me know when and I'll be here," Gene replied.

Both men instinctively looked up even though they were inside the hanger when the sound of a powerful prop plane caught their attention as it made a low pass over the airfield.

"Hey, that's a Merlin!" Conrad said, dropping his wrench and cocking his head a little. "That's a Rolls-Royce Merlin—I'd recognize that deep hum anywhere. And that whistling sound in there...this friend of yours, he's got his hands on some old World War II bird, and with that whistle I'd say it's a P-51! That's the real deal...sends chills up my spine standing here...brings back memories."

"There's no telling with Jeb. He collects a few."

The two men hustled out into the late day sunlight and looked towards the sound of the circling plane.

"Oh my!" was all Conrad could manage to say when it approached the south end of the air strip and slowed.

From the angle where they stood they could see the fighter plane sported a yellow nose, two thick black "D-Day stripes" on the underside of the fuselage just behind the cockpit running below the United States Air Force blue and white star insignia, dark green camouflage on the top half of the plane, and the rest was shiny silver metal.

"I know that paint scheme," Conrad said pointing up at the plane. "I was in Richmond, Virginia in '43…just before Christmas when I joined up with the 361st fighter group of the 8th. We flew into Bottisham Airfield in England. Some of our planes had that paint scheme at first, early in '44, but we dropped the camouflage pretty quick after D-Day. I never thought I'd see that again!"

The P-51 Mustang circled once more and lined up with the runway. The landing gear came down and the pilot brought it in for a soft landing and taxied over to where the two men stood, both smiling from ear to ear. He killed the engine.

"Fellas," Jeb said after sliding the cockpit open.

The propeller was still spinning when Conrad jogged over and tried to scramble his 92 year old body up onto the wing. Gene worried he might break his neck so he went over, grabbed the old man by the hips, and hoisted him up in a quick, powerful toss onto the left wing like he was a bale of hay. Conrad didn't acknowledge the leg-up but took two steps and stuck his head in the cockpit for a look before Jeb had a chance to climb out.

"It's a D, right…a P-51 D? I worked on these back in '44 and '45. She's a beaut! And the paint scheme…I know it…I was a mechanic in the 361st."

"I'm Jeb. Nice to meet you." The pilot held out his hand.

Conrad's trance was broken long enough to shake the man's hand and introduce himself. He immediately went back to looking around the cockpit.

"Here, let me get out and you can climb in," the pilot said. "Is it okay to park here?"

"Oh sure, sure…this is my hanger. I might just take a quick sit in her, since you offered."

"No problem. I've got to talk to that crusty old cowhand over there for a bit, anyway. By the way, I just fixed a coolant leak before flying her down here. Would you have a look around and see if it looks clean."

"Sure I will! They were bad for that, these Merlins. You two go on in the clubhouse over there and make yourselves at home. Nobody's in there, but it's not locked. Make a pot of coffee if you want—Gene knows his way around."

"Thanks, that sounds good to me," he replied.

Jeb climbed out of the cockpit and hopped down off the wing onto the tarmac beside Gene, who was all grins, watching Conrad hard at work scrambling into the cockpit.

"Hey Jeb," the old-timer said pulling himself half way back out of the plane and turning to him with a gleam in his eye. "I gotta ask, why'd you pick this paint scheme? Most guys seem to like the shiny metal all over with those checkerboards on the tail these days."

"The first airplane model I ever made as a kid was exactly like this plane. I was 12. It came with decals and paint and was 'P-51D, serial no. 413926.' I never forgot that plane, so when I had the chance to buy one and have it restored, I didn't have to think twice about how I wanted to paint it up."

"Sheesh, a real nice one, too, if I do say so myself!" Conrad replied nestling back down into the cockpit.

Chapter 14

Vassily Levin's Former House
Wickenburg, Arizona
6:00 p.m.

The memories came rushing back as Vassily walked up his old street in the twilight. When he got to the driveway he stood for a moment looking at the house and it seemed like he should be able to just walk in the door and see Katerina again. He shook off the flood of memories and looked around.

There were several houses on the street, but they were spread out and were set back off the road on several acres of land each. Cars were parked at a couple of the houses, and lights were visible inside some, but nobody was outside to see him as he walked up the road.

Vassily's luck continued; nobody appeared to be home at his old house. He entered the empty car port and walked up to the door that led inside to a utility room. He had no idea what kind of schedule Bob and his wife kept, but it was the time of day for folks to be coming home from work, so he needed to be quick about this. He reached into his pocket and pulled out a key which he had kept in the off-chance he might need to gain access to the house again, and wondered for a moment if Bob had changed the locks.

The key slid easily into the slot on the doorknob and turned.

In a snap, Vassily was inside without needing to force his way in. He closed the door and locked it behind him, then rummaged around the utility room until he found a small hammer. He walked into the guest bedroom and set his computer bag down on the bed and opened the closet door.

"Excellent!" he thought. "It is full of clutter! It may be some time before they know."

Quickly, he pulled out shoes, boots, boxes of old photographs, and a vacuum and climbed into the closet on his hands and knees. He took the hammer and in a back corner began busting holes in the sheetrock. Several blows was all it took to rip an opening large enough to remove a small plastic box, which was hidden between two studs in the wall.

Vassily left the mess inside the closet where it fell but carefully returned all the items back just as he had found them. It was perfect. Even if they discovered the mess, with nothing stolen and no apparent break in, he figured they may not even bother calling the police.

"What do you think, hun...tacos for dinner?"

Vassily heard Bob's unmistakable accent echo down the hall from the kitchen.

"Sure. Sounds good," a woman's voice replied.

Vassily quietly closed the closet door. Footsteps came down the hallway. He stood with his back against the closet door so he couldn't be seen from the open door to the guest room. Vassily's heart raced as he looked over and on the bed saw his black computer bag clearly setting on a white bedspread. Clop, clop, clop...the footsteps came down the hallway right to the doorway and stopped. He heard the woman turn around.

"Bob."

"Yeah, hun?"

There was a long pause....

"Let's not do tacos tonight. Do you mind? Save that for

tomorrow. Let's eat that left over chicken and salad."

"Aw shoot naw, I don't mind, Dear," Bob replied to her. "I'll pull that stuff outta the fridge, then."

Vassily heard her shuffle again by the open doorway and then, clop, clop, clop...continue down the hallway. He took a deep breath. He walked to the window and unlocked it. It slid open easily. He grabbed his computer bag, lowered it by the strap gently out onto the ground and, holding onto the plastic box in one hand, did his best to quietly climb his stiff old body out of the window. He managed to get out landing on two feet without making a big clatter and closed the window behind him. It wouldn't close quite all the way, and he hoped they wouldn't notice it anytime soon.

Vassily grabbed the bag, shouldered it, held onto the plastic box he had just acquired by cradling against his chest with one arm, and snuck around the edge of the house. He walked as quickly as he could down the driveway and up the road. For the second time that day he felt invisible as he simply walked away unnoticed from another potential snag to his mission.

Chapter 15

Harquahala Hills Airpark
Salome, Arizona
6:04 p.m.

"I heard a little about today's news," Gene said over his shoulder as he heaped up the coffee filter with enough dry grounds to accommodate two normal pots.

"Well, I was going to talk to you about something in a day or two anyway, but last night's situation could be related and we have to move fast and carefully on this."

"So what's the scoop?"

Gene poured a pot full of water into the back of the coffee maker, spilling some, and grabbed a few napkins from a holder to sop it up. Jeb leaned back in a chair and drummed his fingers for a moment on the table in front of him.

"It involves some things you're expert on, so I need your opinion."

"Opinion? Jeb, I could have given you that on the phone from the saddle."

"Given the nature of what's going on, it's best we talk across the table. There's been a development."

"Crimeny, will you just get to it?"

"Alright, first, it's back on the air?"

"What is? Oh, you don't mean.... Really? The English Man

on shortwave? After two years of being dormant?"

"Yep."

"I see. Well...that is news, Jeb. Very interesting. And the variant?"

"The first I. D. is spoken, then there's an extra five digit group of numbers read aloud that was not given in the old standard broadcasts, followed by two messages—all numbers in groups of five, and it wraps up with five zeroes. Then 20 more messages are broadcast using the same format but with different I. D.s and the same zeros to close."

"I'm guessing you're receiving this on the old frequency, 6,949 kilohertz, on upper side band?"

"Here's where it gets strange—not that the whole numbers station thing in this day and age isn't strange to begin with. It has been broadcasting on the old frequency, 6,949, but on AM and with greater power, and obviously originating from a different broadcast location, than at any time since we first picked it up in the 70s. It's easily audible in North America. The broadcasts begin at 09:00 and 16:00 UTC. They've been repeating for the past two days, exact same number sequences each time."

"Clearly audible, you say?"

"I'm telling you, Rush Limbaugh hasn't got anything on The English Man on AM at the moment."

"Fascinating."

"Fascinating good, or fascinating bad?"

Gene pulled the pot out from the coffee maker before it had finished brewing and poured the thick, black liquid into two heavy white mugs. The valve on the filter holder leaked and coffee sizzled on the burner as he returned the pot. Then he set one mug in front of Jeb and held his as he took a seat at the table across from him.

"Well, we've been sure The English Man is a Russian numbers station all along," Gene said. "With the fall of the USSR, I was very surprised it kept on broadcasting all those number sequences, especially into the 2000s. There are other means nowadays to quickly and cheaply encrypt messages across the globe. That kind of station requires extensive staff and operational gear to keep running all that time. I guess its main benefit is that with shortwave there is no way to track where messages are sent since anyone with a shortwave radio can tune it in. With texts, e-mails, letters and the like, the recipient is potentially exposed.

"As you know, it's always been a little tricky to pick up The English Man here in the States...certainly possible, especially with good equipment. But, if the broadcasters intend to have an agent receive a message easily with most any small shortwave receiver so that suspicions aren't aroused by stringing up antennas or buying specialized receiving gear then we assumed in the past that The English Man was never intended for general use with agents here in the U. S.

"But if the new signal is unusually strong then it is probably 'fascinating bad.' There's a good chance that someone is reaching out to agents in the field with a very important message, and you sure can't rule out North America now for their target area. There's no doubt the Putinites in Russia these days have their roots in the old Soviet circles. They're acting like they want to return to the good old days of super power status and regroup their lost neighbors together...perhaps this is part of that deal?"

"I've thought of that, but there's evidence pointing in a couple different directions."

"Do tell," Gene said.

"First, I had our buddies in the Navy monitor the signal and see if they could get a bead on it. I also called our friends in Israel to see what they thought about the broadcast's origins. Both came back pinpointing North Africa as the source of the transmissions—specifically Syria. With Russia and Bashar al-Assad being the good buddies they are, it could be the Russians broadcasting again from the new location. They certainly have the funding to do this sort of thing.

"As you know, the map of Syria is peppered with Syrian government forces, Kurdish forces, rebel forces—even Israel occupies the Golan Heights—so no one has yet to confirm for us just whose area that transmission is coming from. I'm sure they must know the exact location of the transmitter by now, but no word on that so far. We know, of course, that it is a very powerful transmitter, and it has been confirmed that the signal is directional and being beamed towards North America. There's nothing subtle about this. Whoever is behind it wants to be certain these messages get to their destinations and doesn't care who is aware that they're being sent. Or, they want it obvious that The English Man is back on the air as some sort of political message."

"Hmm." Gene took a sip of coffee. "Russia has plenty of places to broadcast from back home so you wouldn't think they'd bother with setting something up in Syria with their buddies there. The messages are coded anyway. If they presumably are using the trusty old one-time pad method of encryption to communicate with agents in the field then there is little chance of it being broken. And even if we deciphered the messages, the decryption itself might be in some kind of code—they'd say something cryptic like, 'Make the omelet with cheddar,' that only one specific agent or cell could understand.

"So the real question becomes, if it is Russia, are they wanting to make it seem like somebody else is sending these messages to shift the blame to say, Syria or even ISIL, or maybe just create confusion and throw us off track? Or, maybe it's not Russia at all? If it's not, using The English Man numbers station is a bizarre, twisty way to go about it. Who would even think about that? It's kinda brilliant in a way, now that I think about it. Are you sure it's not us?"

"I should have sent you to the firing squad when I had my chance," Jeb said, pointing a finger at Gene. "Do you reckon it's somebody who knew we would take notice, or is it about getting the message across to agents with certainty—or maybe both? You know, anybody with a laptop or smart phone could find out about The English Man and come up with a ruse like this."

"Yeah, but not everybody could put that kind of transmitter together. If what you say is true, that would take major funding, effort, and the time and space to build and operate a massive transmitter. And without the worry of raising the notice of several very capable international governmental agencies? Hard to say for sure, but my gut says it's about getting the info out to some very special agents. So what other things have you got for me, Mister-Flying-My-P-51D-With-Special-Permission-During-A-Terrorist-Attack?"

Jeb reached inside his World War II pilot's jacket that matched the ambiance of the plane he'd arrived in and pulled out an envelope. He set it on the table in front of Gene and then worked down another sip of coffee from his cup.

Gene rocked back in his chair, removed some papers from the envelope, and unfolded them. His eyes popped wide open and he sat forward again clutching the papers with both hands.

"Son of a biscuit eater!" he said, looking across at Jeb. "We'll that puts things in a different perspective, doesn't it."

Chapter 16

EOD Mobile Unit
Arlington, Virginia
Earlier That Day
3:14 p.m.

Master Chief McAbee was writing up a forensics report on his laptop inside the EOD trailer when the door opened and Officer in Charge Schmitt stepped inside.

"Master Chief, I just found out the Sec Def is coming for a briefing in person. He's on his way."

"Okay, Sir."

"Have we got anything new? Bring me up to...." The OIC didn't get his sentence completed before the door opened behind him and in stepped Secretary of Defense Douglas.

"Attention on deck!" said the Master Chief standing and stiffening to attention.

The two Petty Officers snapped up from their chairs to attention, and OIC Schmitt spun around so hard that he wavered for a moment before catching his balance. Two Joint Chiefs of Staff stood behind the Secretary of Defense, and a third man, clearly a security detail wearing a black suit, sunglasses, and an earpiece, came just inside the door and waited there.

"At ease," the Sec Def said.

McAbee relaxed his posture and stood looking like his normal self. Schmitt, on the other hand, made an attempt to appear more relaxed but by fidgeting slightly just belied his nervousness all the more. The Petty Officers relaxed, but remained standing at their stations facing the officers.

"I decided to come by in person for a briefing," the Sec Def said, speaking to Schmitt and McAbee. "The sensitivity and importance of this matter cannot be over stated, men. I want to stress that this attack is an act of war against the United States and is being treated as such with the full power of the government coming to bear on some type of decisive action in response. I'm going to brief the President again as soon as I leave here, and as you can imagine, this morning's news from you has struck an odd chord. I'm sure you noticed during the press conference that the President withheld the details you provided earlier from the media until you had a chance to more fully investigate the situation. So what do you have for me?"

"Sir, Master Chief McAbee was just about to update me on the latest details when you arrived," Schmitt said. "Proceed, Master Chief."

"Master Chief, it's good to see you again," the Sec Def said with a slight grin. "You look good."

"Thank you Sir," he replied, and gave the senior officer a quick nod, acknowledging the personal greeting. "We've got some solid details to add to what the Lieutenant briefed you on this morning. First, local Police notified us of a video taken by a college student in the Patriot Center parking lot at George Mason University in Fairfax at about 01:20 this morning. When the student heard about the explosion on the news he immediately turned over the video footage, figuring it was of the missile that detonated here. Petty Officer Jackson, would you run the video on the large screen for us."

"Yes, Master Chief," he replied.

The Petty Officer sat down and within a few keystrokes a flat screen monitor on one wall of the trailer began to show the video. The most remarkable aspect of it was the clearly audible eerie chopping noise that droned on. The video itself revealed little more than a shaky light at some distance in the sky. The student's voice was clearly audible speaking to a friend as they marveled at the strange object.

"This was taken at night with a cell phone, and as you can see the only thing visible is a plume of fire in a dark sky at what must be about fifteen hundred feet overhead with a few parking lot lights thrown in which fade the image even more. The audio, however, is very clear. Petty Officer Jackson sent the video over to base to have it enhanced and this is what we received back."

The screen this time showed a faint but clearly outlined image of an aircraft shooting across the night sky. It looked like an airplane with wings and a tail, but attached atop the fuselage from about mid way running back to the vertical stabilizer was a tube. Behind this tube emitted an impressive tongue of fire as it rocketed quickly overhead and then disappeared into the darkness.

"As you can see, Sir, the video substantiates our earlier findings," McAbee continued. "The audio alone is enough to peg this rocket as a pulse jet engine propelled device. The enhanced video clearly shows a rocket of a German World War II era FZG-76 type."

"Okay, Master Chief," the Sec Def said. "What else do we know at this point?"

"We've recovered a few fragments from the missile and I can tell you with certainty, Sir, that this is not a German FZG-76. What we have here is a 10 KhN, which was an early Russian cruise missile—basically a copy of the German V-1, built to spec from the ones they captured at the end of World War II. The 10 KhN had a few improvements, most notably was the addition of a solid fuel rocket booster to assist in takeoff rather than the steam piston system that was part of the launching rail that the Germans originally used. We have found Russian markings on some of the parts we've recovered which clearly indicate it was built in the USSR, most likely some time in the early 1950s."

McAbee turned and looked at the Sec Def and the two Joint Chiefs of Staff accompanying him. No one said anything for several moments as they ruminated on this bizarre twist to an already strange situation.

"Well then," the Sec Def broke the silence, "I guess we've just been attacked by a Soviet Union that no longer exists. Doesn't that just beat all?"

"Sir, if I may add a couple thoughts?" McAbee offered.

"By all means, Master Chief. I'm happy to consider any light you might be able to shed on how we've just been attacked by a Soviet antique, how it got here in the first place, and who it was that engaged us."

"It may not be the easiest thing to hide something as big as a 10KhN, but then again, it is small enough to have been stored in a garage or barn. And, if somehow it could have been hidden for more than six decades and somebody was around who was trained on how to activate it, the shelf life of a rocket like this is phenomenal. As I told the Lieutenant earlier, all it needed to be operational was a launch rail, some regular unleaded gas, an air compressor, and a small battery.

"It's too large to be highly mobile, but it could be moved easily enough on a trailer with a pickup or tractor. I've seen footage of four or five Germans pushing one of these to the launch rail on a big wheeled dolly, so it is possible that a small group, or even a single person, could have managed to launch it, even if it needed to be moved from storage to do so. It's certainly low tech by today's standards, but that works to its advantage in this scenario.

"I've been trying to make sense of all this as we've been

uncovering the facts. Just say, this one was snuck into the country and stashed by the Soviets in the early 50s as an ace up their sleeve—a conventional weapon capable of attacking the U. S. capital. It's not a huge threat by itself. From a military standpoint, there's not much to a single blast of a ton of high explosive. That's not going to put so much as a dent into our military defenses. It's more of a psychological weapon. But if it could be dialed in to hit the White House or the Capitol, it could potentially kill the President or any number of Senators and Congressmen, or if it hit the Pentagon, as we saw with the attacks on 9/11, it is perceived as an attack on the head of our military and could kill military personnel.

"I know the first thing we think when we hear of an attack like this is Islamic extremists...naturally we think 9/11. They are openly at war with us and have vowed to destroy our country and kill us all. Well funded individuals and governments out there are just looking for the opportunity to attack us, especially on our own soil. But, it doesn't add up here. First, there's very little chance they'd spend their energy on putting together an antiquated cold war relic—why would they? The only reason I can think of for the perpetrators to do so would be to throw us off their trail and create confusion, and we know the first thing jihadists would want to do is post a YouTube video of their masked men firing the thing while waving their black flags.

"More importantly, the timing is way off for any garden variety terrorist. If it was intended solely as a terror attack, why launch the missile in the middle of the night when the opportunity to kill people is greatly reduced? Just think how many more deaths would have occurred if it had landed here during the middle of rush hour. Or if it hit any government building, how many more people would die if it detonated during normal business hours. I don't think this is the work of Islamic extremists or homegrown terrorists, which is naturally our first thoughts. They would have gone for maximum casualties and would have timed it for prime time TV. Not to mention they'd be claiming responsibility for it on Twitter minutes after it happened. Add to that that we never picked up one iota of chatter about something this big coming from any source beforehand and it just doesn't add up.

"However, consider the missile itself. If we judge things by its age, it likely would have been planted 15 years before the Cuban Missile Crisis. If the Cold War had turned hot early on, then having it reach and blast D. C. would have made a huge statement at that time. Think about it—the Russians able to bomb our capital in a matter of minutes—suddenly they don't seem half a world away; they're right on our doorsteps and in our minds.

"Still, it seems unlikely that there would be only one missile in such a plan. I've been wondering if there's not a network of such weapons stashed right under our noses. Maybe not all 10KhNs, but other conventional weapons capable of making attacks on other high profile targets in the United States. If so, like with this one, they'd need sleeper agents at the ready to pull the triggers on the order from Moscow. And even though the weapons became quickly outdated in the mid 50s, as tensions ran higher over the next couple of decades, there was no incentive to remove the weapons or the agents assigned to them.

"Quite the contrary, they still were fully functional and well hidden—why not just sit on them and activate them if you needed to? In fact, having a non-nuclear option of attack on the U. S. may have been one more card they wanted to keep up their sleeve. It's pretty bizarre—even unlikely—but it is the one scenario that adds up in my mind given what we're pulling out of that crater outside and what we've seen on that video."

"Well, Master Chief," the Sec Def said, "at least there is no doubt now about what it was that made that crater out there. I'll pass the facts along to the President. In the meantime, let's hope that video doesn't end up on YouTube. The conspiracy theorists will go bonkers and have Hitler alive and well, back from his holiday in South America and up to his old tricks with a stash of old Nazi buzz bombs. Or better yet, Germany is attacking us through a time machine. I agree, it raises extreme concern that there could be more of these relics lying around. Let's hope not. We'll take your thoughts on the matter under consideration. Anything else?"

"Yes Sir," LT Schmitt spoke up, stiffening as he did. "By taking into account the Point of Impact and analyzing the radar data and recorded conversations from the Air Traffic Controllers we have determined a general Point of Origin for the missile. It seems the POO is in West Virginia, most likely in the Moorefield area. The FBI is heading up the search on the ground for the launch site with help from military aircraft and local law enforcement agencies."

"Very well," the Sec Def said, turning on his heel. "Carry on. Contact me straight away if anything new comes to light."

The Sec Def exited the trailer with the other three men in tow. Schmitt looked at McAbee with a furrowed brow.

"Can I help you with something, Sir?" the Master Chief asked, noticing his glare.

"You know the Sec Def?"

"It was some time ago, Sir, but yes our paths have crossed over the years."

Schmitt shook his head in wonderment, turned, and exited the trailer.

Chapter 17

Harquahala Hills Airpark
Salome, Arizona
6:21 p.m.

"That photo in with the papers is a still shot from a video taken by a college kid in Fairfax, Virginia with his cell phone last night at about 01:20 hours," Jeb said.

Gene could hardly believe the image clearly visible in the photo, but there it was right in his hands...a V-1 hurtling through the air.

"Holy bull twinkies, Jeb! Are you telling me that this is what made that crater in the Beltway this morning?"

"The EOD guys on site have confirmed it."

"A German World War II vintage V-1? You've got to be kidding me."

"It's not that simple."

"Simple? How could *that* possibly be simple?"

"If it was a piece of authentic Nazi ordinance then it would be far less politically problematic."

"Oh...you're going to tell me it's Soviet, aren't you?"

"That's what I admire about you, Gene...you're a quick study. It's point of origin was West Virginia."

"I bet they're flipping out at the White House right now. I'd love to be a fly on the wall there to see just how the administration

is going to handle this one. So, you've gotten special permission
to fly out this way during a no-fly blackout across the U. S. to
speak with me in person because you were already looking into
The English Man coming back on the air out-of-the-blue, and
a couple days later an antiquated Soviet buzz bomb successfully
attacks D.C."

"You got it. A matter of national security. And this business
about the 10KhN rocket you see there is highly classified.
Figuring out just what's going on with this mess has top priority.
I was told to take absolutely no risks of this info leaking, and
of course I can't trust the phones on your end. We had to talk
ASAP, so I figured I'd fill up the new bird on the company credit
card and take the opportunity to fly out here for a face-to-face.
I must say, it is something to consider that there's not a single
commercial or private aircraft in the air over the whole country
right now. I didn't see so much as a jet trail up there. Plus, I
missed your coffee. So talk to me. What are you seeing in all
this?"

"Well, this is a complete shocker. Totally bizarre. What
about Putin? Could this be an activation of an old KGB agent?
You know those guys love him."

"You tell me, Gene. This is your area of expertise."

"You're calling me old again, aren't you, you mangy mongrel."
Jeb couldn't help but crack a smile at that one.

"You really have been saving those up for me, haven't you?"

"I'm just getting started. You'll be wanting to leave me alone
so bad before long.... Well, just off the top of my head, Jeb, here's
what pops to mind. For a couple decades, my beat was keeping
an eye on some covert Soviet international operations. I boned
up on all the old MGB stuff—you know, the Ministry of State
Security which they phased out when they instituted the KGB in
1954. Come to think of it, that little interim period just happens
to be right at about the time this V-1 clone would have been

built.

"It seems some inner party power plays were brewing at the time. That helped obscure the big picture of what agents were planted here in those days and what their missions were. Who knows, it's not impossible that someone along the line smuggled that missile in here. I don't think there's any way they could have moved many of that kind of thing into the States, let alone kept them hidden for over 50 years. But one—sure, it's possible. A couple...maybe. Ten...no way. I wouldn't think this is going to be a recurring theme, at least."

Jeb took a quick gulp of coffee from his mug and winced a little.

"So, is there anything you picked up along the way during your very, very long and distinguished career that might point to sleeper agents with this kind of mission being on stand-by?" Jeb asked.

"There you go with the old thing again!" Gene said, cracking a smile himself this time. "Well, maybe. I dun-know. Nothing even close to concrete, for sure. Of course, we'd catch wind about this or that. Some project names would get thrown around here or there that never seemed to surface again. In 1952, we—the CIA I mean—got brought into playing an active role in the Venona project. You know it?"

"Um, that's the counter-intelligence program started by the Army Signal Intelligence Service in the pre-NSA days, right?" Jeb asked.

"Indeed, and it was in operation from 1943 right up until 1980 and wasn't declassified until the mid-90s. One of the best things to come out of its early efforts was the discovery that the Soviet company that made one-time pads for their encrypted messages made a huge blunder."

"One-time pads?" Jeb said rubbing his chin. "Old school cryptology isn't in my bag of tricks. I'm more of a manager who is provided with a secure phone and e-mail account."

"Right...that's why you're here bothering me now with this face-to-face business," Gene retorted.

"Touché." Jeb nodded.

"Anyway, the one-time pads have random numbers on them," Gene explained—his eyes twinkled revealing his love for this part of the game, a fact that Jeb was counting on. "Basically, the letters of the alphabet and the single digits, zero through nine, are given another numerical value. Then the numbers on the pad called the 'key' are either added or subtracted to each one. If both the sender and receiver have the same page of random numbers then viola! They can undo the simple math correctly and communicate. If that page is then torn out and burned and never used again, the encryption is essentially unbreakable because the key to encrypted messages is forever a moving target and totally random. But, making truly random lists of numbers isn't an easy business. If you get sloppy and reuse the same number sequences for the key then the brainiacs in a group like Venona can figure out your messages—or at least parts of them."

Gene shrugged and then took a gulp of his thick black brew.

"So with the Nazis breathing down their necks in Moscow at that time during World War Two, I guess it was easy for the Russians to try and cut corners and this company produced around 35,000 pages of duplicate random numbers."

"How do you know all this stuff?" Jeb asked, shaking his head.

"I investigated all kinds of info about my pet projects over the years—I had to have something to do while I was on the clock up by the Beltway besides read my *Quarter Horse Journals*," Gene shot back, chuckling.

"Yeah, but you remember it all," Jeb replied. "That's what gets me."

"So, long story short, this guy, Lieutenant Richard Hallock, was working on breaking coded messages linked to Soviet trade traffic at the end of World War Two. He was the first to realize they'd doubled up on their one-time-pad keys. One of the messages that they decoded because of Hallock's discovery led them to figure out that the Soviets had espionage agents in the Manhattan Project in 1946. The interesting thing here, though, is that duplicate one-time pad pages continued to be used by the Russians, reportedly at least as late as 1948. But, I found out it went on longer than that. I had a look at several partial decrypts from about the time the CIA was brought into Venona, which again puts us at 1952 or '53, about the time this V-1 clone would have been produced. It's a real long shot, but I'd have these new messages checked to see if they could be decrypted using those old duplicate pads since they are from roughly the same time as that missile."

Gene picked up the stack of papers on the table and shuffled the photo behind the others. There were five pages of white copy paper covered with columns and rows of seemingly random numbers.

"These are those new English Man broadcasts?" Gene asked.

"Yep. Those are all the ones they've sent since they started broadcasting again. They are being repeated at intervals around the clock. I thought it wouldn't hurt for you to have copies of them in case you have a flash of genius, or, *much* more likely, some of that incredible Gene Davis good luck."

"It's skill, baby...it's all skill!" Gene shot back with a grin.

Chapter 18

Town of Wickenburg Public Library
Wickenburg, Arizona
7:30 p.m.

Vassily had not walked so many miles at one time in years
as he had that afternoon. Renewed purpose in life had proven
to be a massive stimulant for the old man putting a spring in
his step. Being outside in the fresh air and sunlight for a change
had increased his pep as well, and his mind had focused on how
best to achieve his objectives as he strode along the roads and
sidewalks.

Vassily figured that by now the staff from Casa del Sol had
to be aware of his disappearance and would have notified the
authorities. He needed to get out of sight. He needed to get on
with things

The physical realities of the day, however, caught up with
him all at once that evening as he walked back into Wickenburg
from his old house on the outskirts of town. A sudden fatigue
overcame him, and he looked around for a quiet spot to sit and
sort things out.

Dusk had fallen and little remained of the day but a slight
glow off to the west where the sun had faded below the horizon
beneath an otherwise black sky dotted with stars. Street lamps
illuminated the sidewalks as the cool evening air descended upon

the town. Vassily saw the public library ahead, half a block away. He dragged himself over to one of two inviting benches near the front entrance and plopped himself down.

At least his boots were a custom made pair so they had been especially kind to his old feet, he thought. He made himself comfortable and resisted the urge to flop right over for a nap on the bench. He was ready to sign into a hotel for the night, regroup, and order something to eat.

Vassily placed the plastic box he'd retrieved from his old house on his lap. He inhaled deeply, exhaled slowly, and popped it open. Every few years he had opened up that wall in the closet, updated everything, and repaired and repainted the sheetrock so that no one would ever be suspicious that it held his secrets. Sure, two decades had passed since he had been contacted by his handlers, but that was the thing—they had never contacted him to deactivate him. So, he kept up his end of the bargain, just in case.

On top lay a small digital, AM/FM/Shortwave travel radio, about the size of a paperback book. He lifted it out and set it on the bench beside him. Next was his Makarov pistol in a shoulder holster, the service pistol he had worn when he had "defected" to the west. Oh, what an amazing show that whole defection scheme had been...a great plan concocted by his comrades. Khrushschev himself, he had been told, had approved it.

Vassily had flown out of the Soviet Union to Iran in 1961 in a Sukhoi Su-9, one of the most cutting edge Soviet jet fighters at that time—one which had only two years earlier set the world's altitude and speed records. The hope was that no one would guess that he was a double agent. How could he be? After all, surely the Soviets would protect this fighter jet technology with the utmost care and not let one simply fall into American hands, even for such a trick.

The truth, Vassily knew, was that the Su-9 was no different

internally than its predecessor, a developmental jet called the T-3. Soviet agents had discovered that the Americans had acquired plans and intelligence on the T-3's internal makeup. Only the exterior of the Su-9 differed from the T-3, and this was observable in any decent photograph, which the Americans surely had plenty of. This being the case, and hoping that the Americans did not know that they knew about the T-3 information leak, it had been decided that the jet might be a very useful tool to establish Vassily's credibility in the west.

At first, the scheme seemed to be moving along nicely. Within 24 hours of his landing in Abadan, Iran, the jet was whisked away by the Foreign Technology Division of the Department of Defense and was in the U.S. He was on American soil a day later, cooperating, answering questions, being granted asylum, and talking about how much he was sick of vodka and drab concrete buildings. His Soviet counterparts were busy faking a calculated freak-out. They produced the expected number of high level communications among themselves about the defection and made stern demands through certain channels that Vassily and the jet be returned to them immediately.

Considering what he had done for them, the Americans had been more than happy to let the Russian pilot enjoy asylum in the States, drink fine wines on their tab, and keep his service pistol as well. But, the original plan, to get the Americans to allow him to use his talents to work as a test pilot for military aircraft and thereby feed information back to the USSR, ultimately had failed. It had been a high stakes gamble giving the U.S. an Su-9 to play with, even if the technology was known to them, and they had lost that roll of the dice.

Vassily had feverishly attempted for a decade to get into some aspect of test piloting or otherwise working with cutting edge military aircraft. While he had made some friends from those circles who went to bat for him, the higher-ups voices of caution ultimately had shot down his attempts at landing a job working with the latest military aircraft technologies. However, he had been able to work as a pilot in the private sector for his livelihood and for pay that was dazzling to the ex-Soviet military man.

Always true to his original mission and a way of life he knew was superior to the ghastly bi-polar nature of capitalism with its shrinking numbers of super wealthy and growing masses of poor and struggling "middle classes," he had been unable to acquire any information valuable enough to warrant the risk of being caught sending it back home. Even so, there was a plan B for him...a plan "just in case things get hot," which he was uniquely qualified to undertake.

Underneath the pistol and a full box of matching ammunition were an unopened bar of soap in a box, a variety of documents, a magnifying glass, and $4000 in bundles of recent 50 and 100 dollar bills. The papers included two Russian passports, each had his photo and a different alias. The passports he had renewed once every ten years simply by sending new photos of himself to an American address through the mail. A few weeks later, the new passports came in the mail as if by magic from different addresses within the U.S. to a post office box he had rented in the name of one of his aliases in Phoenix.

There also were matching New Mexico drivers licenses for the aliases which he had kept up to date, likewise via the mail along with an American credit card for each alias. The credit cards were a complete mystery to him. They arrived to his P. O. box from the credit card companies just randomly, staying up to date over the years though he never did anything to renew them. Clearly somebody out there must be looking out for things, or else this all somehow was on autopilot from years ago—Vassily had no idea.

The old man placed two 50s and a 100 in his wallet along with one of the New Mexico drivers licenses and the matching credit card in the name of Aleksandr Ivanovich Kuznetsov. The passport in that name he tucked into his suit coat inner breast pocket. The license and credit cards in his real name he placed into the plastic box along with the other documents, pistol, ammunition, and radio. The bar of soap and magnifying glass he put into his computer bag.

It was then he saw the flashing lights reflecting off the buildings around him.

"Oh no, the police," he thought. It would be extremely bad timing to be caught with the contents of the box he was carrying. He heard a vehicle coming down the street from behind him. His mind raced for a good story to get out of being pegged for the old Russian guy who had gone AWOL from the old folks home—he couldn't think of one right off.

Vassily peered out to the street as best as he could without turning his head to get a look at the oncoming vehicle. It was a Wickenburg marked police car. It was slowing down.

The old man sat paralyzed wishing he had continued another block or two where there were hotels he could check into and get off the street. The siren wailed as it approached him, and Vassily nearly jumped off the bench, but as the car reached the library where he sat, it sped off. With lights flashing and siren wailing it disappeared down the road past him.

He stood cradling the box with one arm and shouldered his laptop bag again with the other, the adrenaline causing him to shake. He got his legs moving again and walked as fast as he could down the street. The tremors from his sudden fright finally subsided and he ducked into the lobby of the first hotel he came to.

"Hel-lo," he said in his thick, slow speech with his Russian accent to the young woman at the counter. "I vrould like a vroom for zee night."

Aleksandr Ivanovich Kuznetsov placed his credit card on the counter. A few minutes later he was heading to room 9 with his key card in his hand and a big smile on his face.

Chapter 19

The Point of Origin
Hardy County, West Virginia
11:15 p.m.

Sheriff Bradley Jones had climbed up the steep mountain side with only a flashlight beam slicing into the darkness to see for himself what his deputies had found. The FBI was on the way, but he had been asked to secure the area until they could get there. As inaccessible as the site was it secured itself, but given the nature of the events that day, he was not taking any chances. He had his whole department on the clock to help keep an eye on things. He also had been asked by the feds to make a report by phone immediately to the EOD mobile command in Arlington about his initial findings at the scene. The EOD team would coordinate the new information with what they were finding at the blast site.

There was no cell service near the area, so after looking around he hiked back down to his car and drove eight miles to where he had a signal to make the call.

"Master Chief Rick McAbee, EOD Mobile command," a solid voice came over the phone.

"Master Chief McAbee—Sheriff Jones, Hardy County, West Virginia here," he replied. "I was told to report to you immediately if we found the launch site. Well, we found it."

"Yes sir, Sheriff. We'd like to have any details you can provide."

"Well," Jones scratched his head as he tried to figure out where to start, "the site is very remote, way up in the mountains. It is right in the area that your satellite surveillance pegged for us. First, I should tell you we have a body."

"A body?" McAbee echoed. "Really?"

"Yes. An older gentleman. I'd guess he's in his 80s. It's too early to know for sure, but I'd say it was a heart attack that killed him—there's no signs of injury or struggle or any indication that it might have been a homicide. And he's been here awhile, probably 18 to 36 hours."

"I see," McAbee said. "Any chance he had an I. D. on him?"

"I'm afraid we're not that lucky," the sheriff said. "But I expect we'll hear something pretty quick about an elderly fellow missing if he's from around here in West Virginia. The rest of this deal...let me tell you, I've seen some stuff in my time but this is totally bizarre."

"I can imagine. Just try to give me any details you can—anything might be helpful."

"Of course," the sheriff said. "This site is way up on a rock face of a mountain. There is a little ledge there and on the ledge is a flat car—like a small train car on tracks. There is a rusty metal rail set up like a ramp mounted on top of the flat car pointed out to the east. It isn't very long; only about 25 or 30 feet, a little longer than the car itself which must be about 15 feet long, but up on that mountain side anything launched from there would be 1,000 feet above the valley floor and at least 3,000 feet above sea level already.

"There are a couple of metal doors that open out of the cliff face where this ledge juts out. It's an old mine of some kind. It looks to me like this fella used a hand winch to crank that flat car out of the mine on the tracks, like it was just sitting in there ready to pull out and go. It'll be a lot easier to see what's what in the daylight, but I have no doubt that this is where your missile launched. There was just the one flat car. No other weapons are around that we've discovered. Not much of anything else inside or outside of that doorway to report. The rest of the area is just rocky mountain sides and woods."

"Can you describe any of the equipment for me?" McAbee asked.

"Well, I looked around best I could with the flashlight," the sheriff answered. "First, the body was down the hill some distance from the flat car and ramp. Lying beside the body was a control panel looking type of deal. It was black and about the size of a briefcase with some switches and dials on it, but really old looking stuff. It's not digital or anything like that. It kinda reminds me of my grandfather's old radio he kept in the den from the 40s. It was connected by a cable to another console on the flat car. There was a five gallon gas can at the scene. It was shiny new red plastic, so I'm guessing he brought that with him. It was empty but I opened it and gave a whiff and it definitely smelled like gasoline. If it had been full, that would have been a heck of a lot of wieght for the old fella to pack up the mountain—it's a wonder he made it to the site with it, and no wonder that he had a heart attack.

"There was a backpack outfitted with some batteries—all modern looking stuff in the backpack. There also was a little air compressor on the ground by the flat car, the kind you plug into a cigarette lighter. Inside the doors to the mine there wasn't much else, really. I took some photos with my cell. They're not great with the flash and all, but it'll give you an early idea of what the scene looks like at least. I'll send them to you as soon as I hang up. Send them to this number?"

"Sure, that'll be great, Sheriff. Thanks for the help."

"No problem. I'm no expert, but by the looks of things in the cave there, this flat car and old electronics had been there a long, long time. Any idea what we're looking at here?"

"I'm not at liberty to say, sheriff," McAbee replied. "We're working to figure out just what is going on here, and what you've told me has been helpful. Please make sure you and your guys keep it under your hats for now while we gather the facts. This is a matter of national security, you understand."

"Will do, Master Chief. Will do. Anything to help you find whoever is behind this deal."

The men hung up. A moment later McAbee's phone buzzed. He opened up a text message with three photos. In the first he could make out a launch rail attached to a flat car. The second showed an empty tunnel entrance with two metal tracks on the ground leading into it. The third was of the body of an old man on his back, eyes still open, his face looking oddly serene.

McAbee pressed a number on his phone and put it to his ear.

"Hello, Lieutenant Schmitt here," came through the speaker.

"Sir, it's McAbee. We have the POO site. You'll want to come and see a few photos for yourself. And, there's a body at the scene."

Chapter 20

Harquahala Hills Airpark
Salome, Arizona
7:05 p.m.

"One more thought," Gene said to Jeb.

Jeb still sat across the table from him, leaning back in his chair. The pilot courageously downed a gulp of coffee sludge from his cup as he listened to Gene.

"We can't forget that it was the age of McCarthy," Gene continued. "So the hunt for commies was on all across the country—it was a craze. If the Soviets were going to do something like sneak in some cruise missiles, it would have taken extreme secrecy to pull it off.

"I don't know," Jeb interjected. "Especially back then, the borders were wide open in long stretches. And we have reports a decade later of the Russians even using rockets from aircraft to launch weapons and other things into the country along the coasts to their operatives—although that was never confirmed."

"Well, if it did happen, something of this scale," Gene asserted, "very, very few people could have known about it. It seems extremely improbable, but I suppose it's not impossible. Man, if something like that has happened, just think of it... keeping a buzz bomb and the agent to operate it off everybody's radar for 65 years! Nobody talked. Nobody made a million on a book deal about it after the iron curtain rusted away. Nobody traded the info about it for cash to the U.S. government. Sheesh! That might just be the best kept secret of the Cold War, and that agent is hard core dedicated."

"I do find it far fetched," Jeb said sitting up straight in his chair. "And why, if it wasn't something they activated over the course of the entire cold war and beyond, would they use it now?"

"Well, that's pretty self explanatory, Jeb," Gene said in earnest. "It's way wackier out there now than it ever was during the cold war. The good old days of cold war stability are gone, after all. Now it's Russia and Iran getting all cozy and provoking everybody. And with Putin annexing Crimea and flying into everybody's airspace taunting them and buzzing our Navy ships with fighters, it really doesn't seem all that far fetched to me that they might do this just to stir the pot."

"I don't know," Jeb said.

"After all, without proof they did it the Russians can simply deny knowledge and involvement and laugh themselves silly for the free pot-shot they got to take at D.C.," Gene said. "Heck, a few hundred yards to the north and it sounds like that thing would have landed at good ol' Cafe Ground Zero right there in the central courtyard of the Pentagon, for crying out loud."

"Flying into our airspace over the ocean is one thing," Jeb said, "or even taking a close dry run at a destroyer in international waters, but firing on our capital with a ton of high explosives is an act of war. That's stepping way over the line—everybody understands that difference."

"Well, I wouldn't put it past Putin," Gene continued. "I really wouldn't. And as long as I'm talking off the top of my head, if there was some operation involving sleeper agents and buzz bombs from back in the day, once it was in place, there really was no need to fuss with it. In fact, it became more dangerous all the time to dismantle it even if they wanted to with the ever increasing ability we have to gather information— satellite imagery, double agents, and such. Imagine trying to explain dismantling a long-hidden buzz bomb to our authorities. They might have thought it was better to just let that operation lie like a sleeping dog; if nobody ever says anything, then there's no barking and nothing needs to be done."

"Um," Jeb said, seemingly unconvinced.

"Now that the USSR has fallen apart, all the easier," Gene continued following his line of thought. "If a Soviet V-1 surfaces because someone stumbles across it, blame it on the old guys, deny any knowledge of it, and it'll make interesting headlines for a week. But if they got caught trying to get rid of it, then there would be major suspicion stirred up about what other such devices they have hidden around the country. By design, there was no need to contact the sleeper agent or agents until they were activated. These guys, if they exist, or did exist, were not here to find and send back information, after all. They probably would have been assigned to a mission and would've just waited for the word in case one day they were activated."

Jeb took another run at his coffee, wincing a little as he swallowed.

"I don't know," Gene shook his head and chuckled as he continued, "more than 60 years later, and long after the fall of the Soviet Union...man, that's some seriously crazy stuff. Maybe some old KGB official who used to be right at the top who's about to die decided he'd play his cards for the heck of it. The V in V-1 was for vengeance, after all. If his old sleeper and his antique ordinance just happened to still be alive and ticking, that could have produced today's attack. It sounds insane, I know, but it's gonna take loco to explain loco, my friend. And this photo... now that's about as crazy as it gets!"

"You're *not* wrong there, my friend," Jeb said, getting up from the table. "I gotta get going. There's one more thing I need you to do."

"No, no...I don't like the sound of that, Jeb. I know that tone."

"With everything at stake, I hope you'll understand the urgency here...and your country needs you, Gene."

"Oh man, you're not going to ask me this are you? My first week of retirement, Jeb. Re-Ty-Urd...retired! Done. Home. Not dealing with bureaucracy. Got cows to brand with a happy crew of new friends. I already missed supper tonight because of you."

"You know I wouldn't ask if it wasn't the most extreme circumstances. A missile landed in D.C., for crying out loud. We gotta move on this, and we can't afford mistakes. You know that. You might be the one who can get to the bottom of this extremely weird situation, cowboy, with those old Russian contacts of yours."

"Geeze Louise...how bad is it going to be?" Gene asked shaking and hanging his head simultaneously. "Go ahead, ask me."

"You'll need to fly via military cargo plane to Frankfurt. Drive out to Davis-Monthan Air Force Base over in Tucson tonight and you'll have the thrill of riding in the backseat of an F-15 E Strike Eagle if you promise not to touch any of the blinking things there in the back seat. There will be one filled up and waiting to take you to Andrews in Maryland where you'll catch your ride to Germany. From there you can take a regular commercial flight to Moscow."

"Can't you get me one of those exceptions you're using so I can fly a Cessna from here down to Tucson instead of spending three hours in the truck after a really long day on the ranch?"

"Sorry friend, no-can-do," Jeb said shaking his head and walking swiftly towards the door. "You're *retired* so there's no way to get those papers shuffled during an emergency like this."

"You cotton pickin,' pickle headed....that is such Bolshevik...!"

Jeb hastily slipped through the door to avoid catching the brunt of the snowballing tirade Gene flung at him from across the room—it was a doosey.

Chapter 21

Super 8 Motel
Room 9
Wickenburg, Arizona
1:51 a.m.

Beep! Beep! Beep!

The pulsing electronic tone did not compute to Vassily at first.

Beep! Beep! Beep! Beep!

"What is that?" his mind wondered. "Where is it?"

Beep! Beep! Beep!

"Where am I?"

The noise seemed very distant in the darkness of his confused mind. Incrementally he began to awaken to slivers of consciousness from the complete blackness of a sleep that was more like a coma than his normal slumber. The fatigue from the previous day with its extreme excitement and excessive exercise had worn him down.

Slowly, his mind began to recognize that the monotonous beeping was an alarm clock on the table beside the bed. He rolled over and peered into the darkness trying to get his bearings. No, he was not home. He was not in his room at *the* home. He was in a hotel, he remembered.

Vassily flung the covers back, sat up on the edge of the bed, and felt around for the lamp switch. Click. The light flooded the darkness. He began randomly pushing buttons on the clock until it finally quit beeping. The red digital display read 1:53 a.m.

The old man shot up out of bed, slipped his suit coat on over his white tee shirt to serve as a robe, since he only had the clothes he had worn the day before, and sat down in a chair by a small table.

On the table lay the letter he had received from England. Beside it was a pad of hotel stationary that he had found in a drawer, a plastic ballpoint pen that had been in his computer bag, and the shortwave radio that had been in the box from his house.

Vassily read the letter again:

Dear Mr. Levin,

Congratulations! You have won an all expense paid trip to Greece!

Please call our offices between October 9 and October 11 for details between the hours of 9:00 a.m. and 4:00 p.m. Your winner's authentication number is: 6949.

Have a wonderful day!

The old man had checked before he went to bed to be sure; yesterday had been October 10th, so today was October 11th. How lucky that he had received his letter in time, he thought. He turned on the radio. A steady low hiss of noise emanated from it. He peered at the digital display and punched buttons until it read 6,949 kHz, the frequency indicated by the "authentication number" in the letter. Still nothing but a stream of noise came from the speaker. A glance at the clock by the bed revealed that it was 1:57 a.m. He turned the radio up a little more, moved its small telescoping antenna around, and glanced back at the clock.

1:57 a.m. seemed to last forever. He kept watching the red display expecting it to change. Finally...1:58. He went over the math again in his head to be sure. Wickenburg, Arizona did not go on daylight savings time. That being the case, Greenwich Mean Time always should be seven hours ahead of Wickenburg. He knew the times on the letter he received would be stated in GMT, so 09:00 GMT minus seven meant 02:00 hours in Wickenburg, or 2:00 a.m. So that should be any moment now.

He could have waited until the next broadcast at 4:00 p.m. (or, 1600 GMT), a much more reasonable 9:00 a.m. local time for him, he mused. But, to get this message as soon as possible interrupting his comatic sleep was worth it. The atmospheric conditions could be unpredictable for shortwave transmissions, as well, so he figured he had best do all he could to receive that message at his first opportunity. He would get better radio gear only if absolutely necessary since that carried with it a much greater potential of arousing suspicion and would cost him more time.

He glanced at the clock again, 1:58. Still nothing but the hiss of an empty channel filled the room. He waited. Then, finally, clearly over the speaker came a mechanical male voice speaking slowly in English—an odd automated voice that Vassily thought sounded like a computer with an American voice attempting to speak with an English accent—"Zero, nine, five...zero, nine, five...zero, nine, five. One. Zero, nine, five...zero, nine, five.... zero, nine, five. One. Zero, nine, five...."

Vassily shuddered and his hair bristled all over his body. This broadcast really was for him, his call number being 095. Only the oldest agents of the sleeper class carried a zero designation at the front of their call signs. They were very rarely used since they were sleeper agents, after all. Plus they had been set up in foreign countries many decades ago as operatives of the Soviet Union, so he figured many of them were no longer alive.

"Zero, nine, five...zero, nine, five...zero, nine, five. One. Zero, nine, five...zero, nine, five....zero, nine, five...."

As Vassily heard his number 095 emitting from the radio as clear as day, he sat up straight and swelled with pride.

The "one" added to the message intro between the three repetitions of his call number indicated that he would have one message in this transmission which would follow after the next section of the message, the "preamble," which was read twice.

The old spy reflected on how much more difficult it had been in the past to tune in the station on the rare occasions he would get messages. He always had managed with a travel type of radio, but once he had to string up a long wire out the window to a barn and attach it to the antenna to boost the signal. As always, the transmissions would be broadcast again at 20 and 40 minutes after the hour of the initial broadcast to help agents get the message if reception was poor, but there would be no need for that this time. The station was crystal clear—by far the best he had ever heard any of the Soviet numbers stations.

The voice said, "Zero, nine, five. One," and then paused for an extra few moments. Vassily glanced at the clock and saw it blip to 2:02.

Then the voice on the radio began again, "Seven, two, seven... two, six...seven, two, seven...two, six...." Then there was another extended pause.

Vassily jotted down, " 727, 26," at the top of the page and then with his pen at the ready he hovered over his pad ready to write.

The voice began again, "Two, five, eight, seven, four...two, nine, one, six, three...zero, nine, eight, one, nine...."

Vassily scribbled the numbers down onto the pad.

Chapter 22

East Bound Interstate 10
West of Phoenix, Arizona
11:15 p.m.

The thought of postponing the rest of the first branding on his new place to travel half way around the world grated on Gene's nerves, even if it was for extraordinary circumstances. He had passed the torch of that old life onto others now, and he could not believe he was getting sucked back in, and so soon.

The cows and horses were on his mind even as they receded further and further into the dark of his rear view mirror. He longed to be catching a few hours of sleep and then awakening to the smell of bacon frying and strong coffee brewing in the ranch house before heading out into the cool pre-dawn to saddle up Dusty for the day. But instead, he was in his pick up truck in the middle of the night cruising along arrow-straight Interstate 10, and he was beat.

Bruce alone had remained at the house when he had returned to the ranch. The capable cook had said not to worry about the sudden change of plans. He had offered to call the rest of the crew and line them up to finish branding the following week. That would work—he just needed to get this mission over with and get back to where they had left off. It would certainly give him much to look forward to.

Gene looked out to the right and saw the green sign for "Exit 109, Sun Valley Pkwy, Palo Verde Road" near Buckeye, Arizona, reflecting the light of his high beams back at him. There were two things that passing this exit always brought to his mind— antique war birds and the oddity of the Palo Verde nuclear power plant.

Buckeye had a nice municipal airport just a couple miles off the Interstate from the exit—a nice long runway with a decent asphalt surface. No commercial carriers used the airport so it was reasonably busy with only general aviation traffic, which was his kind of airport. He had flown in and out of there many times when he had been scoping out this area for his ranch. Plus, there was an aviation museum attached to the airfield which he liked.

The museum owned quite a few old war birds including a General Motors TBM-3E Avenger torpedo bomber. That plane was the kind that the Navy's youngest pilot President George H.W. Bush had been shot down in while attacking the Japanese on the island of Chichi Jima during World War II. As one Navy pilot to another, Gene had relished the opportunity to visit with the President about that experience on the few occasions when they had met over the years. The future President being rescued by an American submarine from the Pacific waters after bailing out remained the detail that Gene found most astonishing about the ordeal.

Once a year the Buckeye airport put on an air show which drew a big crowd, and a bunch of really nice war birds always flew in for the event. Gene had flown in for this "Air Fair" the past several years in a row while he had been meeting with real estate agents and then finalizing the details for the Lazy G. He was looking forward to going every year now that he was retired.

"Humph...retired!" he grunted aloud to himself, breaking the silence in the pickup.

This year, he had heard a rumor than one of the few flying

B-17s still in existence, Sentimental Journey, which was based over in Mesa, Arizona, at Falcon Field, was going to be there. Aside from loving the great nose art on this plane, Betty Grable in a pin-up pose, Gene was a huge B-17 fan. This was quite odd since he had only flown fighters and small private aircraft while in service and out, and wasn't nearly as interested in large bombers. But the B-17 held a special place in his heart anyway, and he really wasn't sure why. He wondered about it while he drove along. Maybe it was how his heart weakened when he climbed into one for a look.

It is one thing to fly into combat with the speed and maneuverability of a jet fighter like he had, or even the prop fighters of the age earlier than his own service. But to see how men faced long bombing missions in open, unpressurized planes at more than 30,000 feet with the wind blowing in open waist gunner doors with temperatures plummeting to 30 below zero, and knowing that flak and fighters would be seeking to punch holes through their thin metal skins to hit the vital organs of both the men and the machines as they rumbled along...whew, it took his breath away just to think about it. He had a great admiration for the men who did that job, and continued to get it done through such tremendously difficult circumstances to win the war against the Nazis.

The B-17 certainly was an elegant plane quite unique in its design lines, too, he thought. And so many of the "flying fortresses" had continued to bring their crews back home even after devastating damage—he'd seen photos of B-17s with gaping holes through the fuselage, most of their tails missing, whole sections of wings shot off, and so on still in the air and flying for home—that he just loved the famed machines. Older planes often seemed like living creatures to Gene, with individual personalities and propensities, and the B-17 was one of the most alive of them all in his mind.

That air show was coming up soon, Gene suddenly remembered. He would have to check online and make sure he was back from Moscow in time to go pick up Conrad and fly over for the day in his two-seater open cockpit bi-plane, a Boeing Stearman Keydet Trainer that he had bought a few years back.

Gene passed the exit and as he did some lights in the distance caught his eye. On the same road that the Buckeye airport was on, just past it a few miles, was the Palo Verde Nuclear Generating Station. The lights gave away the gigantic plant's position in the darkness. In the daylight it was easy to see the massive plant from the Interstate.

When Gene had first seen it, he had found it incredibly strange that the largest power plant in the United States by net generation was this nuclear power plant located out in the desert. He had checked into it after seeing it from the air flying into Buckeye the first time, wondering how a nuclear power station could possibly be in the desert? After all, they require water to cool the reactors, so weren't these things always near huge bodies of water? He had been amazed to discover that Palo Verde is the only nuclear power plant in the world that is not located near a large body of water, and that they got around that situation by evaporating water from the treated sewage of nearby cities to cool the reactors.

"Now that's an interesting marriage of technologies," Gene thought.

The miles slipped by as Gene left Buckeye behind him accompanied only by the stars shining brightly in the night sky. His thoughts turned from war planes, nuclear power stations, and livestock to the puzzle Jeb had handed him.

"A flipping Soviet made V-1!" he said aloud, and shook his head.

Gene tried to make sense of it. There seemed to be very little likelihood anyone would have gone to the trouble to build an authentic buzz bomb replica to attack D.C. these days. That would be an extreme effort to undertake for a ruse, and to what end? Who would bother pinning the blame for an attack on the U.S. on the former Soviet Union? Gene couldn't think of a single scenario where that made sense.

And if somebody could get that much high explosive together inside the U.S., it seems much more likely that a truck bomb would be the way to go. It certainly would have been more accurate. Plus, if present day terrorists could sneak weaponry as huge as a V-1 into the country, surely they would have gone with something a little more modern and more accurate.

The likelihood of an old buzz bomb being on the international arms market was zero, too. As impossible as it seemed, it was much more likely that this was an authentic antique that had been armed and hiding inside the U.S. since the early days of the cold war.

"Hmmm," he said aloud, wondering if the old missile could have been set up to go at a moment's notice all these years? Perhaps fueled up and on the launch rail ready for the press of a button, and it just suddenly went off accidentally? No, there were too many steps needed to get one of those pulse jet missiles into the air. At the very least, the gas would have to be recent to be a viable fuel and a battery of some kind would have to be charged up, he figured.

Gene took a swig of warm black coffee from his plastic thermal cup. The dash lights were bright enough that he could see "Fly Navy" with a silver set of wings underneath printed on the side of the cup. He passed a tractor trailer.

Back to square one, he thought, and proceeded to kick the facts around in his head again as he approached the lights of Phoenix. The English Man was back on the air. After being off the air for a couple of years, the station came back and at a much higher power than before. Same frequency, with the same configuration of sets of numbers read aloud in English, but it was unmistakable that someone had put quite a bit of money and effort into making sure that these new messages definitely got through to North America.

It had to be related. An old Soviet numbers station comes back on the air and within a few days an old Soviet cruise missile strikes near D.C.—those were the only two facts that lined up and made sense in the otherwise dreadfully nonsensical situation.

So, what about the old communist guys? What about Putin? Could they/he be planning something big and this was just their idea of a fun pre-cursor? Gene wouldn't put it past them, but only if they had the upper hand and were really about to drop a sledge hammer. He couldn't see any possible way that they could have the U.S. in that kind of checkmate.

On second thought, scratch that—if they did have a plan to flex their muscles in a big way, launching an old V-1 seemed completely unlikely, even for that bunch, Gene thought. They'd probably fly a hypersonic PAK-DA strategic bomber straight over North America at five times the speed of sound and dare us to catch it to show off their advanced weaponry and antagonize us before they'd actually bomb us with an antique—again, what's the point?

The numbers station messages just might be the key. Is it impossible to decrypt them, he wondered? Maybe, probably...he continued the conversation in his head. If there were only some way to find out more about how they fit into this bizarre attack. Gene had one old contact in Moscow in particular who might be able to shed some light on that; Jeb hadn't been wrong on that point.

He thought about his research on many of the old numbers station messages over the years, and The English Man station in particular. Not a single word had been decrypted in the hundreds of messages that he had studied in recent decades. But it captivated him every time he held a printed copy of the columns of digits from a numbers station broadcast. Right there in his hand was a message; he simply could not access its information.

Hmmm...but wait, he thought, he may not be able to decode these new messages, but what if...?

Gene picked up his cell phone from the console, flipped it open, dialed Jeb's number, put it on speaker phone, and set it down again while he drove.

"Hello?" came the groggy sound of Jeb's voice.

"Jeb, it's Gene."

"Gene...it's late."

"Yeah, I know. And I know you know I know because, guess what? That's right; instead of catching some shut-eye like your lazy carcass, I'm driving to an air force base in the middle of the night after working all day branding cattle on my new ranch to go on a very special vacation after retiring last week, Jeb. That's how I know."

"Right, right...touché cowboy. Did you call me for a reason or just to make me pay for reminding you that your country needs your special talents?"

"These messages you delivered...."

"Yeah?"

"Two things...first, they begin with a three, then a two digit number sequence."

"Okay, Gene, that's great, a real breakthrough."

"Listen, we have been pretty sure that those intros indicate right up front who the messages are intended for. It stands to reason that they are not in code. In other words, the agent's assigned number is not coded because the agent would need to know that a particular message is for him or her, right? So each agent is assigned a number which is code enough for that part."

"Like 007."

"Exactly, Jeb. And you would be 000—a big fat bunch of

zeros! So, get some of those interns searching the archives for any other messages that begin with the same first set of numbers as these new ones. Go back to 1960."

"That stuff is in boxes in some basement somewhere, I'm sure. It could take forever."

"Get cranking on it. And, any word on exactly where they were sent from yet?"

"Um...nothing new since we spoke. You on your cell?"

"Yes, yes, I know...but I need you to do whatever you have to, and right away on this in particular. Call your buddies at the Navy, in Israel, at the CIA, in Germany, call your crazy psychic aunt Clara in Sedona; and get a bead on exactly where...I mean get photos of the place if you can. This should be doable somehow. We'll *parlez-vous* when I get back. I'll come to you on my way home...and I emphasize here for your benefit, *on my way home*!"

"Alrighty then. Will do—in fact, I'll make a couple of calls right now. Have fun on your vacation! I hear Tahiti is amazing this time of year."

"Kiss my grits you...."

Jeb took the cue and hung up.

Gene flipped his phone shut and rubbed his right temple. This was all starting to make his head hurt. He turned on the radio and hit shuffle on his I-pod. By the luck of the draw, Willy started singing, "On the Road Again." How appropriate, Gene thought, and sped ahead towards Phoenix.

Chapter 23

Super 8 Motel
Room 9
Wickenburg, Arizona
2:11 a.m.

Vassily experienced no trouble jotting down the stream of numbers as they were spoken by the semi-robotic "English Man" without missing a single digit.

After his agent number "095" had been spoken over a couple of minutes at the beginning of the transmission and then the preamble "727, 26" was heard, the message had been a sequence of seemingly random numbers spoken in groups of five digits. To mark the end of the message, "000" was spoken twice. When the broadcast went silent, Vassily leaned back in his chair and looked at what he had scrawled on the pad:

```
095
727, 26
25874 29163 09819 84679 14854
97508 36685 13334 37591 56206
17028 40313 33440 86870 48998
84605 44922 36987 35298 07680
90008 60264 52814 81925 44890
42139 34345 39236 51615 20644
```

49373 04999 77288 27325 93997
52769 86282 92649 59349 00726
13046 62774 70184 38098
000, 000

There it was, the long awaited message that nearly had come too late in his life for him to do anything about. He soaked in this moment. Decades spent waiting, pretending, and integrating into the enemy's society now unexpectedly paying off. Everything seemed to be clicking into place and the culmination of his entire life's work sat there before him represented in a handful of numbers scribbled onto a piece of paper on the table in front of him. It seemed rather short for something so monumental. Now it was time for the next stage of the operation, decryption.

Vassily stood and walked over to the dresser. His computer bag leaned against the television that sat on top of it. He shifted the laptop and shuffled things around in the bag until he located the bar of soap still in its original box and the magnifying glass that had been in the plastic box he had retrieved from his old house. Taking them out, he returned to his seat at the table.

Vassily removed the soap from the box and carefully examined it. He felt in his jacket pocket for his old worn pocket knife, found it, and opened the smaller of its two blades. Along the edge of the soap he made out a faint fine line. He placed the sharp edge of the knife along the fracture. He wiggled the blade slightly working it into the line until the soap popped apart into two halves revealing a secret compartment inside.

Within the soap was hidden a very tiny pad of paper. On the top sheet could be seen minute print, too small for him to read clearly. Vassily grabbed his magnifying glass and peered through it at the top page. He was able to make out lists of numbers, organized into sets of five in two columns.

This "one-time pad" was Vassily's key to knowing what his

radio message said. He had received several messages over the years, but nothing since the Soviet Union had crumbled. Each message had been decoded by using the top sheet of his pad, which he then tore off and burned. Then the next page of the pad was ready for whenever he received another message. His handlers on the other end had a copy of the same pad. Since these two pads were the only ones with identical random number sequences, his messages could be encrypted by them and decrypted by him, and by all accounts it was impossible for anyone else to figure out the random key numbers to unravel the code.

Vassily eagerly got to work to see what the message said. He had a twinge of fear that someone on the other end after so many years might have the wrong pad or perhaps even the wrong sheet of the right pad, and the numbers would remain just a bunch of truly random nonsense. Everything was riding on this. Using the magnifying glass to read them, he wrote the random numbers from the tiny pad directly underneath the first line of numbers from the message.

25874 29163 09819 84679 14854
26844 79958 85809 52670 92803

The sender had produced the message's numbers by taking a series of digits that represent letters and numbers and then adding the line of random numbers from the one-time pad using a special process called "modular addition." Vassily now would undo this math to get the deciphered digits of the original message.

Modular addition for his message was achieved by simply adding each number of the original message to its corresponding random number from the one-time pad and writing the sum, but if the sum was greater than nine, only the second digit of the sum was written. So in modular addition, three plus four equals seven (3+4=7), but nine plus eight also equals seven (9+8=7).

Vassily began his subtraction:

2-2=0, 5-6=-1....

After subtracting only the first five segments, Vassily couldn't wait any longer. He had to see if the text would make sense. He took the first line of subtracted numbers that he had written across his pad and began the final phase of decoding it. This was simply a matter of associating every two digits with either a letter or a number. The key to that part of the puzzle was to take the English alphabet, A to Z, assigning A as 1 (or 01 to give it two digits), then B was 02, C was 03, and so on to Z which was 26. Then the numbers 0 through 9 carried on after, so 0 was 27, 1 was 28, up to 9 which was 36. The first line of the message after subtracting the random numbers from his tiny pad now read:

09030 50215 24010 32009 22051

These he split into two-digit numbers and prepared to set the associated letter or number underneath each:

09 03 05 02 15 24 01 03 20 09 22 05 1

The old man felt a flutter in his chest and his mind raced after only the first letter, I, was written under its corresponding number, 09. His mission's name was "Icebox," and when he wrote C underneath 03 his shaking became barely controllable. ("You're not acting very professional, old man," he thought to himself.) Then he went for broke and finished out the whole line:

09 03 05 02 15 24 01 03 20 09 22 05 1

I C E B O X A C T I V E

That was it! That was the phrase he had waited for...his mission was active.

He quickly went through the math for the rest of the message. He paused to look at all the numbers before he divided them up into pairs.

97508 36685 13334 37591 56206
17028 40313 33440 86870 48998
84605 44922 36987 35298 07680
90008 60264 52814 81925 44890
42139 34345 39236 51615 20644
49373 04999 77288 27325 93997
52769 86282 92649 59349 00726
13046 62774 70184 38098

Deciphered, the whole message was in English and read:

ICEBOX ACTIVE PROCEED TO CACHE 54 PROCURE
RA115 CONTACT IS 037 CODEWORD BUTTERFLY
THEN PROCEED TO FLUSHING 26 OCT 1200 TARGET
WALL STREET XXX

Vassily tore the tiny top page off the one-time pad. The old man chuckled because in the distant past he remembered deciphering a message in a hotel room not unlike this one, but he had lit a match and burned the paper in the ashtray. That wouldn't work now. Not only was there no ashtray but he didn't have matches or a lighter as a non-smoker these days. He figured with smoking being banned from hotel rooms that burning it would set off some fire alarm. Instead, he crumpled the tiny sheet, walked into the bathroom, and flushed it down the toilet.

Chapter 24

Aragvi Restaurant
Moscow, Russia
10:15 p.m.

"Oh, John Wayne! Look at you, cowboy."

The woman's British accent did not belie her Russian roots as she approached the table where Gene sat in a red leather chair directly across from the bar under an arched ceiling. It was hard for him to believe that only half a day earlier he had been in Arizona. His speedy military transport to Frankfurt, Germany, and catching his commercial flight for the last leg of the trip on time allowed him now to sit a world away in Moscow for a late dinner—it was a complete time warp.

Gene smiled wide, stood, and walked around the end of the table behind his date. He gently positioned her heavy, red leather chair as she took a seat. The Aragvi Restaurant on Tverskaya Street was a fitting place for this reunion. Gene had been surprised to see it had reopened but was happy for the nostalgia of the place.

"Anna, you look ravishing as always," Gene replied, returning to his place at the table, removing his cowboy hat and placing it upside down in the chair beside him. "Much too classy for an old cow hand like me. The years have treated you well."

"*Gene*, you make me blush!" she replied, smiling coyly.

"Ah, I see...when did you find out?" he asked.

"Decades ago," she answered.

The woman's hair was shoulder length, now silver, but gentle curls still presented a most pleasant girlish effect. But it was her eyes that always slayed Gene. They were a most extraordinary color—a hue that he had never encountered in another person and that he could only classify as grulla, an unusual coat color found in some Quarter Horses.

Those eyes instantly took him back to Milan, Tel Aviv, Prague...and Paris. Gene remembered vividly that in those days Anna's hair had been the exact same grulla color as her eyes. His cover had nearly slipped his mind just at the sight of her the first time they met, and every time thereafter, as well.

"I see," he said. "Well, Aglaya...."

At the uttering of her real name the woman across the table shot him a warm, playful glance, and her now thin lips curled to a smile.

"...I haven't known of your background nearly as long as you have mine, I'll admit," Gene said, "but you are aptly named, 'Beauty.'"

"Oh Gene...but how nice that in retirement we can let go of the pretense, eh?"

"Indeed! But perhaps I need to call you Anna again, just once more."

"And here I thought we'd finally get our moment. There is just something about the rugged, independent American cowboy that makes a girl swoon. How is the ranch going, by the way?"

"If I didn't know better, Aglaya, I'd think you were keeping tabs on me."

"Well, it's been a while since I was in the saddle—English was always my style—but I'd love to try riding Western for a change."

"I tell you what, come visit and I will show you the time of your life. Plenty of horses, cows, open spaces, and big skies.

The truth is, I was only on the place a week before my country needed me again...and here I thought the nation would run just fine without me. Seems you and I, we're of a bygone era, but apparently we're still critical to the operation."

"Perhaps I'll visit you, Gene. I'd like that very much. But for now, I'll help you out this time just so we'll be even. It's nice to have the chance to settle up."

Gene smiled at the thought of the insanity of past times. And while he never expected he would miss the Cold War, those times seemed simple and even in a way far less dangerous when compared to the current mess the world was in.

"Anna, seeing you is the only perk to this invasion of my retirement."

Gene looked at the menu.

"Well look at this," he said, "they even have my favorites from before, *khinkali* and *khachapuri*. Hard to believe some things still survive."

"It is, is it not?" Anna replied.

The two old acquaintances enjoyed a meal together. In that old cellar-like restaurant for a time, the modern world faded from view and the past again came to life. They reminisced, and Gene realized how few people in the world could understand those years of his life the way this adversary could. They finished eating and slowly the present asserted itself back into their consciousnesses.

"Aglaya, you can do one thing for me," Gene asked. "I figure if anybody can help me get to the bottom of this, it's you."

"Well Gene, your timing is quite revealing you know. What a shame a lass can't just be the draw for a fella...but of course I'll see what I can do for old time's sake. What are you looking for?"

Gene looked right into Aglaya's amazing eyes as he spoke quietly.

"It's funny you know?"

"What's that, cowboy?"

"There's hardly a person in the world I'd share this with...."

"Oh, do tell."

"I mean, here I am in Russia at the Aragvi about to give a woman I've known to be a hostile foreign operative for years some of the most highly sensitive information in the world right now."

"Sounds exciting! And, I can't remember the last time I was called *hostile*."

Gene gave a grunt at her remark and they both laughed heartily. Then Gene leaned towards her. She took the cue and likewise drew towards him across the small table.

"It was Soviet...not just Soviet, but really old school," he spoke to her in a whisper. "I'm talking early 50s."

"What...the missile in D.C.?" she blurted out quietly.

"Yes," he replied. "Had to have been sitting hidden forever, but still viable. Which means the personnel had to be available, trained, and in place. Either there was a very old sleeper still on duty and he got switched on, or someone else came across some very old top secret info and had the means to use it. The English Man is very busy. It makes me wonder if he has other plans to visit my country. I can provide whatever you require to obtain anything helpful here. And honestly, I just want to get back to branding my cows, so you'll be doing me a huge favor. I'm staying at the Lotte, room 210."

"Times are very different now," Aglaya sighed. "But one thing about it...money is king in ways it never was before here in Russia. It is a pity, really. I do miss those tough, old, ideological comrades. Oh well.... [She sighed.] There may be something I can get for you, but it will be expensive."

"No need to economize, Aglaya. I'm spending other people's money, and you better carve yourself out a queen sized commission or I may just come back here and scold you."

"Now that *is* tempting, Gene. Quite!"

Chapter 25

EOD Mobile Unit
Arlington, Virginia
5:12 a.m.

Master Chief McAbee stood outside the EOD mobile unit at the edge of the blacktop overlooking the crater, drinking a cup of coffee, and gazing at the sky with its hint of glow to the east beyond the city lights of Washington, D.C. It was much like his experience the previous morning except that flames no longer danced in the pit and no plume of smoke rose over the scene before him.

The few hours of sleep he had managed to get had helped his general disposition. He was about to get started collecting the details that had been piling up overnight for a meeting with Lieutenant Schmitt in an hour.

The moon was nowhere to be seen, so McAbee gazed up and noticed how some stars still shown brilliantly in the night sky even with the city lights glowing around him. He was wondering when the truth of the origin of the missile would be made public and what reaction it would....

An enormous flash illuminated the sky in the distance to his left which drew his eye. Two heartbeats later:

BOOM!

The sound and concussion hit him simultaneously. Instinctively, he had ducked and put up his free hand and the other holding the coffee cup between his face and the fireball in the sky. The blast had been so bright it had cast long, eerie shadows for several moments all around him and inside the crater. Just as quickly, it had become dark and silent again. He stood back up and peered up at the sky looking for any signs of jet fighters in the air.

A second later, people jumped out of trailers all around the command center area. They ran here and there fairly crazed, looking up, and their chaotic voices filled the air. But, the show was over as quickly as it had begun and now there was nothing to see. McAbee had been the only one outside in the area to witness the massive aerial explosion.

Before he could decide what to do next, a great welling roar filled the air, the ground shook, and the whole world trembled. McAbee's mind, long programmed to think tactically, was tricked only a moment before it registered that two F-16s had made a low pass overhead, hightailing it somewhere.

The men on watch from the EOD mobile unit now were outside the trailer standing around the Master Chief. Many people were lying flat on the blacktop, just beginning to raise their heads for a look around.

"Well boys," McAbee said, shaking his head and speaking loudly enough to overcome the ringing in his ears, "some pilots obviously had the need and clearance to hot-dog-it right over D.C. I'm guessing from the size of the explosion that they may have shot down another one of these missiles over to the north there."

People were getting back on their feet and running all around the poorly lit command center area shouting as a general flurry of activity set in.

The Navy crew looked wide-eyed but steadily at the Master Chief.

"Alright, inside and back to work," he said. "First, Petty Officer Howard, get on the phone to command and get a report on what just happened. Petty Officer Davies, get a fresh pot of coffee on...we're going to need it!"

Chapter 26

Super 8 Motel
Wickenburg, Arizona
4:45 a.m.

Vassily wasn't certain how much time remained before the staff at the Casa del Sol Community convinced the Police that he had really disappeared and wasn't just wandering around the grounds somewhere. That may already have happened the previous night—he hoped not.

Regardless of whether they would be worried that he was senile and wandering the streets of Wickenburg or that his disappearance was for some other more troubling reason, the result would be local news media involvement with his face plastered all over the television. He needed to get as far away as possible immediately and not be recognized in the mean time.

That realization got Vassily thinking about the television for the first time since he'd been in the room. He found the remote and switched it on. He checked all the main channels which were running news of a second missile attack on Washington, D.C. Vassily had not yet heard about the first one.

"Air traffic has been resumed for all airports east of the Mississippi at this hour even though a second missile apparently was intercepted by American fighter jets and shot down just a short time ago over the nation's capital," a news anchor said. "We go live now to Washington, D.C. for the latest."

"It's just after daybreak here outside of the Pentagon in Arlington, Virginia, Sherry," a reporter said to the anchor, holding his microphone, a slight breeze blowing his hair. "You can see behind me the massive damage caused by yesterday's missile attack. It will be months at the earliest before this section of 395 can be rebuilt and be back in operation. But the breaking news is that a fireball appeared in the sky just before dawn inside the beltway somewhere over northwest Washington, D.C. Early reports indicate U.S. fighter jets intercepted a missile, or perhaps an aircraft, but no injuries or property damage have been reported so far."

Vassily grinned when the camera panned past the shoulder of the reporter and showed a great crater in the earth illuminated by the glow of the early morning light, with gnarled concrete, black top, and rebar strewn about like piles of strange confetti.

"Oh my, of course!" the old agent said aloud.

Only at that moment had he connected the dots and realized what was happening. The numbers station message...his mission being activated...of course! These attacks were the work of other sleeper agents like him. They all were being activated. People must be assuming these attacks were the work of terrorists, he thought But no...it wasn't terrorists. It was happening!

"The question everyone is asking is if this was indeed a scud missile attack, as is being widely speculated," the reporter continued, "and if the explosion overhead this morning was another scud being intercepted and destroyed by an American air-to-air missile. Also, the question is being asked across the country, how is it possible that America can be attacked by large conventional missiles right here at home? These medium range weapons must have been launched from somewhere within the United States, quite close to D.C. But, still no response from the White House or the Pentagon as yet regarding the type of missile used in either attack or who may be responsible for this act of war against the United States."

Vassily's heart swelled with pride and hope. He had to get going.

It was still very early, but he was wide awake. The realization that he was activated was thrilling. This whole unbelievable turn of events right at the autumn of his days had been an incredible salve for his aging body. Even with all the walking and other stresses of the previous day, he felt good. The Revolution was getting back on track. The old Soviet guard was resurging and, yes, there were assets like him still ready to fight against the true evil of this world. And he knew that something big had to be coming behind these operatives fulfilling their missions.

He had no idea what the big picture might be, but he knew a new wind was blowing to the west from Russia. In fact, in this era of unbridled corporate capitalist excess, Marx was needed more than ever, and he was lucky enough to be chosen to attack at the very heart of it. His mission might be the death blow to the central nervous system of American globalization and capitalism. The old man smiled and thought, may it never recover from the coming might of his mission alone.

Now that air traffic was resumed to the western half of the country, even though it was very early, no one would suspect it was strange if he checked out of the hotel and called a cab to get to the airport in Phoenix for an early flight. There was no time to delay now that things were heating up. The time line must be kept.

The old man loaded his pistol and put his holster on over his shoulders. The arrangement would conceal the Makarov nicely under his suit jacket. His mission was active now so he was sanctioned to use any means necessary to carry it out. He would succeed, even if he was 82 years old. He gathered his few belongings and went to the hotel's lobby.

Through the automated sliding glass doors at the hotel's entrance, Vassily could see it was still dark outside. He turned in his room's key card and checked out at the front desk. He asked the young woman behind the counter about getting a shuttle to the airport in Phoenix.

"It's too early for the shuttle," she said with a smile. "For early flights we can call you a cab."

"Yes, fine, zank you," Vassily replied with his obvious Russian accent.

He took a seat on a chair that faced the main doors and provided him a view of the loading zone out front. There were a couple of the previous day's newspapers on a table beside him with large front page photos of the devastation in Washington D.C. A television was up on one wall in the corner playing the morning news.

Only five minutes passed before lights flickered against the doors and a yellow cab stopped right out front. The next sequence of events happened so smoothly that Vassily marveled at how well his training had been ingrained in him in his younger years.

The old man stood up and strapped his computer bag on over his shoulder and cradled his plastic box in his left arm.

The television was on a local news segment. It was easily audible in the room. A blond woman news announcer said, "and in Wickenburg, police are looking for 82 year old Vassily Levin who went missing from the Casa del Sol Retirement Community yesterday...."

A big photo of Vassily's face came onto the screen just as he took his first step towards the door.

The receptionist looked up at the television.

Vassily squinted as he turned and scrutinized her face.

Her eyes popped wide when she saw the photo on the television. She looked at Vassily as he walked slowly towards the door.

"He has a Russian accent...," the TV announcer continued.

Vassily slid his right hand underneath his suit jacket.

The receptionist frowned and looked back at the television to the photo for another glance. She had enough time to know for certain it was him before she spoke questioningly....

"Hey mister?" she called, her brow still wrinkled in a frown of confusion.

Without breaking stride, Vassily deftly took ahold of the pistol grip, swung it out, aimed it at her, and pulled the trigger.

Crack! Crack!

Two shots rang out in quick succession. The bullets manufactured half a world away, half a century before, pierced her twice through the chest.

She fell.

The automatic doors swung open. Vassily reholstered his Makarov and exited.

The driver was just getting out of his cab. He stood up, looked across the roof of the car towards the glass doors which now slid closed automatically, and he saw the old man approaching. Vassily smiled and walked calmly to the cab. The driver, seeing the old man was going to get the car door for himself and had no luggage to put in the trunk, climbed back in and sat down behind the wheel. Vassily got into the rear passenger side of the cab and said, "Phoenix please."

"You going to the airport?" the driver asked.

"Vrell yes...I have a flight."

"Very well."

The cab pulled away from the hotel. Vassily noticed the faint smell of burnt gunpowder which quickly was overwhelmed by the odor of what could only be burnt truck stop coffee as the driver took a big swig from a tall Styrofoam cup.

Chapter 27

Room 201, Lotte Hotel
Moscow, Russia
Noon

Gene sat in the splendor of his hotel suite in a cushy chair. The place was extravagant to the extreme, even boasting a baby grand piano in one of the spacious rooms. The South Koreans, who owned this hotel chain, obviously did luxury to a point that made him somewhat uncomfortable, and he longed for the rustic setting of his ranch house.

He had turned the chair so that it faced away from a large window—the amazing panorama it displayed was too distracting. The view overlooked the modern Arbat District of Moscow, a scene that seemed both familiar to him, with the grand Novinskiy Boulevard running past the hotel and the equally broad Moskva River flowing in parallel just past it, and oddly unfamiliar, with the colorful, cheerful, free moving busyness of a city he remembered as gray, lifeless, and decaying. The ornate five-star furnishings everywhere in the suite, from the intricately patterned carpet to the vaulted ceilings with fancy trim, also were distracting to him, but not as bad as looking out of that window.

Throughout the first half of his career, Gene could not have imagined that the Cold War world would cease to exist in his lifetime, and certainly not have unraveled so soon after Reagan's presidency. Being in Moscow, and especially making contact with Anna again, had him a bit reflective.

Overall, it was pleasant for him to sit in a modern Moscow and think that the work he had done had helped secure the increased freedoms the Russian people now enjoyed. Of course, no "real" Russian would agree with his perspective, but he really did not care about anyone else's acknowledgement of his work over the years. Just seeing the Arbat area of the city transformed into a truly thriving financial, shopping, and artistic district was proof enough of improvement over that dismal past for him.

"Okay," Gene thought. "Enough of that."

He had to shift mental gears now. His own country was at risk. He was in Moscow for a reason and he needed to concentrate.

Gene looked more closely at the papers Jeb had handed off to him at the airfield back in Arizona. The sheets showed long columns of seemingly random numbers in groups of five digits that had been broadcast recently by the English Man.

Flipping through the pages to see if anything might jump out at him—even though experience had taught him that with transcriptions of numbers station numbers, nothing ever did—Gene again rehashed what he knew of the current situation.

The attack on D.C. clearly indicated that active operations were afoot and somebody was not afraid to pull the trigger. People had died. A section of Interstate 395 and other roads were now a massive hole in the ground, and all this was in sight of the Pentagon. Not to mention that attacking Washington D.C. was an unquestionable act of war certain to provoke no small retaliation. Of course, the list of people who would like to do this was long, but who had the resources?

As for the missile, it was known to be a V-1 type, an antique, and Soviet built. And the English Man was again on the air, with greater strength than ever with long messages like the ones he was staring at, which had been broadcast just before this attack. All of this certainly pointed the finger at the Russians. In fact, it looked conclusive according to the evidence alone.

But all that just seemed too tidy to him. Either the Russians had such impunity these days that they wanted to smack Uncle Sam right in the face, which seemed unlikely to Gene, or was somebody else framing the Russians?

What did the Russians have to gain by such a crazy stunt, after all? Sending a fighter pilot to hotdog 50 feet off the bow of a destroyer in international waters is one thing, but to attack the U.S. capital from inside the country? Well, that's biting off a whole lot more than Gene believed even the Russians wanted to chew.

Plus, their usual game tended to be double-speak diplomacy. This attack really did not allow the opportunity for them to make some weird case to the international community or to deny that it even happened. He just couldn't see what the Russians had to gain if they were behind it other than just trying to get away with a serious attack that could somehow be explained away by pinning it on the old Soviet state officials, all while laughing themselves silly behind closed doors and giving the U.S. a headache. No, the repercussions would be too extreme even for them to stomach merely for a good laugh at the U.S.'s expense.

If it were somebody else wanting to frame the Russians...that could fit into this scenario. But just how in the world did they get their hands on an authentic antique Soviet buzzbomb and sneak it into the hills of West Virginia? That was just way too bizarre to be plausible.

Or perhaps—Gene grabbed his chin as he mulled it over—could the Russians be using this bizarre attack to case the joint? It could be a means to do extensive research on U.S. readiness and response to a missile attack on D.C. Using an old missile and sleeper agent would keep us working to figure out just what exactly was going on thus delaying any retaliatory response.

It was a great ruse...but then again, why not use a more modern missile and blame it on ISIS or Iran? Or, North Korea, or China?

"Or the Ukraine," he interjected aloud to himself thinking about all the lies Russia had spun about its neighbor recently, and laughed at his own joke.

The bottom line was that Gene's gut told him there would be other attacks, even though there had been a delay following this one—what, two days now? No, only one day and some hours, he realized. He had covered enough distance in that time that it seemed more like a week. Further, he had not checked the headlines in hours, so for all he knew more could have happened. He thought about turning on the television, but the stillness was too enjoyable and conducive to thought. He stared again at the random numbers on the papers in his hands.

A knock on the door startled Gene back into reality. He placed the papers in his brief case and closed the lid before standing and walking into another room. He opened the door to find a waiter hovering over a fancy meal cart.

"Room service," the waiter said.

"I didn't order anything," Gene replied, looking at the waiter across the cart in the hallway. "There must be a mistake."

"No sir, Mr. Davis, this is definitely for you," he replied in English with a slight Russian accent. "Complimentary."

From the look the waiter shot him, Gene had no doubt it was true.

"Oh, well yes, please bring it in—I am hungry," he said.

Gene tipped the man and then had a look around the cart. The waiter removed a silver dome from over the entre.

"Roasted, smoked salmon with buckwheat and dill from the Ovo," he said.

Gene knew that the Ovo was a famous Italian restaurant

located somewhere in the sprawling hotel, but he had not eaten there before.

"It looks magnificent," Gene said. "Thank you."

"It is my pleasure, sir."

The man left the room and Gene began inspecting the cart more carefully. Everything seemed just-so, but when he moved the silverware off of a white linen napkin and unfolded it, a folded piece of paper fell out onto the tray. He opened it.

It contained three lines of numbers. Obviously Anna had something for him and this was a bank routing number, an account number, and a sum which he could assume was in U. S. dollars, "and that certainly should include her commission," he thought.

Gene, not one to let a good salmon fillet go to waste, went ahead and enjoyed his lunch and then left the room. He took the stairs down rather than the elevator, went through the main lobby, and exited out onto the street. One nice thing about the Lotte Hotel was that it was only two miles from the U.S. Embassy. He took his time ambling along and thinking about his cows and how much he would rather be under the sprawling sky of Arizona, boots in the sand, than in a city...any city...let alone one half way around the world from home walking on concrete.

Gene recognized an old familiar sixth-sense feeling overcome him. Somebody was right behind him. As a reflex, he decided to whip around quickly and offer his hand to introduce himself to throw whoever it was off guard. He took one more step and spun around to the left while extending his right hand as he went.

Sure enough, a man in a long black coat was right behind him. As he pivoted around and faced him, right hand held out to greet him, Gene said, "Здравствуйте товариш!" a fluent "Hello, comrade!" in Russian.

The man was caught completely off guard by the sudden move just an instant before he was going to make contact with

Gene. But Gene also experienced a shock to discover that rather than grabbing the man's hand to shake, he felt the cold metal of a pistol barrel.

The sheer shock of feeling a gun in his hand made Gene grasp it and twist. It was an accidental move, a complete reflex—Gene, in all honesty, was about the farthest thing from James Bond when it came to gun wielding and hand-to-hand combat—and the man was so flabbergasted at Gene's sudden spin-around and fluent Russian greeting that he simply let go of his grip on the pistol.

Instinctively, Gene with the pistol now in his hand repositioned it from one hand to the other and stood pointing the barrel at the man's abdomen. The two faced off for just a few ticks of the clock. Then Gene smiled from ear to ear, looking calmly into the man's brown eyes that were as wide as saucers.

Chapter 28

EOD Mobile Unit
Arlington, Virginia
7:30 a.m.

"Okay, Master Chief," Lieutenant Schmitt said, having just arrived for the work day. "What do we know?"

"Overnight, we recovered more small pieces from the missile used in yesterday's attack," McAbee answered. "These new pieces are consistent with the original findings, that the missile was a 10KhN, pulse jet propelled Soviet manufactured V-1 type of weapon. Our team in West Virginia also found conclusive evidence of this—namely the launch rail, control panels, gasoline container, small compressor, and such. We can say with certainty that this is an original 10KhN missile stored on-site in a mountain mine shaft for a very long time and apparently launched yesterday by an old man who was found dead at the launch site. He remains unidentified at this hour, but it has been confirmed that he died of a heart attack. So, no big surprises overnight with any part of the investigation."

"And this more recent incident?" Schmitt asked. "What was that all about?"

"We have received word from the SecDef's office that another missile was launched against D.C.," McAbee said. "The in-bound missile was intercepted and shot down by our fighters. It had been on a south-easterly course, which puts the point-of-origin most likely in Maryland. No word yet as to the exact nature of that weapon except that, like the one that detonated here, it seems to have been conventional. We have orders to investigate it as soon as the areas where any debris landed have been ascertained and secured by local law enforcement. I expect some of those should be reported to us by mid-day."

"Very well, then," Schmitt said. "I hear you saw the excitement this morning first-hand."

"I did," McAbee replied. "I have no doubt that the missile I saw shot down by our fighters was at least as powerful as what caused the crater here. We received a report that says the pilot shot down the bogey with an AIM-9X sidewinder missile using infrared homing—so heat-seeking was used to target the missile, and it was an easy kill. Apparently there was no radar guidance system detected on the incoming missile. It sounds to me like it easily could have been another one of these doodlebugs."

"O-K...I'll brief the SecDef on where we stand here," Schmitt replied. "As soon as the locations in the debris field from the second missile come in, take a petty officer and get working on them right away."

"Will do," the Master Chief replied.

Chapter 29

I-17, Northbound
Phoenix, Arizona
8:35 a.m.

The old man welcomed the green of pine trees as he drove
north from Phoenix towards Flagstaff leaving the high desert with
its saguaro cacti and vast spreads of sand and rocks behind.

He had asked the cab driver to take him to the American
Airlines departure terminal at the Phoenix Sky Harbor Airport.
He paid the driver in cash, gave him a nice tip, smiled and made a
quick comment about having missed a flight to L.A. the previous
day with the airports being shut down and having to stay in the
hotel overnight.

As the cab pulled away, he entered the airport. People—no
doubt still stranded trying to head east—were standing around
everywhere, lying on the floors in corners, and occupying most
of the available seats. Every television had a crowd around it
watching the latest news about the attacks. Vassily made his way
down an escalator to the baggage claim area.

The place was abuzz with the flow of people from the
morning arrivals pouring into the area around the shiny metal
baggage carousels. He pushed through the crowd and exited
through the doors leading to the free shuttle bus service that ran
to the airport's massive rental car facility several miles away—

an island of a place with every imaginable rental car company represented.

The shuttle took about five minutes. The bus was packed with people and luggage, and luckily Vassily had managed to get a seat. It pulled up to the curb out in front of the main entrance to the rental car building. He stepped off the bus and entered the building and looked at a long line of counters with the many different company signs hung above them. He chose the one with the shortest line, but with a flurry of early business flights coming in and no flights going east, they all were crowded. One even had a hand-written sign taped to the front of the counter that read, "NO CARS AVAILABLE."

Due to the unfortunate business back at the hotel, his first choice of aliases was blown. For the rental car, he provided the other credit card and matching New Mexico driver's license with the more American sounding name: Steven Harper. He hoped this would not stand out to the same extent on paper that a name like Kuznetsov would.

"Please, call me Steve," he said flirtingly to the young woman behind the counter as he presented her the credit card and I.D.

She smiled and keyed his numbers into the computer. The printer spit out a few documents, they chatted, he signed them, and off he went down an enormous escalator to the huge parking garage to get his rental car. It went flawlessly.

A quick stop at a Wal-Mart a few blocks off of Interstate 17 allowed him to pay cash for some clothes, a small suitcase, food, and some bottled water. He hit a drive-through for two sausage biscuits and coffee, and off he went to the north.

At Flagstaff, he picked up I-40 and headed east.

Chapter 30

Novinskiy Boulevard
Moscow, Russia
1:19 P. M.

A black four-door Mercedes whipped up to the curb near
Gene and the man whom he now held at gun point. The darkly
tinted window on the rear passenger's door lowered. Gene
noticed a sharp prodding in his back—another man had come up
behind him and was impressing upon him the fact that he had a
gun, as well.

"Mr. Davis," came a husky voice with a Russian accent from
the car, "would you care to join me, sir?"

"This is a little dramatic, don't you think?" Gene replied.

Gene maintained a big grin while looking right into the cold
stare of the man in front of him. The grin finally morphed into
more of a smirk. He remained focused on the man's eyes, finger
on the trigger. A moment passed where everything just hung
there, paused in a stalemate. Gene relaxed his posture, spun the
handgun around into his other hand, and returned it butt first to
its owner.

"We mean you no harm," the voice said, "but merely wish to
impress upon you the extent of your options."

"Point taken," Gene replied.

He turned towards the car, stepped up to it, removed his

cowboy hat so that he could climb in without whacking it on the top of the car's doorway, and took a seat in the back of the car beside an older gentleman in a suit. One of the men outside closed the door behind him. The driver glanced back at Gene in the rear view mirror and then looked ahead peering out of the windshield.

"Eugene Davis," the man beside him said, "I'm Victor Nikolayevich."

"I see. Well, apparently you are already acquainted with me—so Mr. Nikolayevich, who are you?"

"Yes, Mr. Davis, let's just say it is my job to know all about important visitors who travel to our lovely country. It is nice of you to come and celebrate your retirement here with us in Moscow this week."

Gene smiled. Apparently half of Russia was celebrating his retirement, he thought to himself, first Anna and now this guy. He didn't enjoy this kind of recognition from his colleagues back home.

"Well, I don't know about being very important, Mr. Nikolayevich, but then with as much as you know about me already, you must know how I loved Moscow back in the old days. Once I retired, I just had to come to see the changes for myself."

"That must be a very strong passion to get you here given the grounding of all commercial flights from your country. Quite a feat, really."

Gene squinted and looked right into the man's eyes, sizing him up. Clearly Mr. Victor Nikolayevich had good intelligence on him.

"No, you've got that wrong, friend," Gene said. "I just flew in from Frankfurt."

Nikolayevich's lips curled slightly upwards in his own smirky kind of smile.

"Indeed, that is true, Mr. Davis, but you know what I mean. Let's not beat around this bush, eh? And let me put you at ease...I'm here to assist you."

"Assist me? That's great!" Gene replied. "I'm indeed relieved to hear it. So, aside from greeting me at gun point, in what capacity do you see yourself helping me, Mr. Nikolayevich?"

"Oh please, you must call me Victor."

"Right, Victor. So?"

"I am going to give you a suggestion."

"A suggestion? You know, this city has changed enough since I was here last that I could certainly use a couple of suggestions about the best places to check out while I'm in town."

"I'm going to suggest to you that things are rarely as they seem in this world today," Victor said. "And while it is certainly flattering that you'd want to come straight away to celebrate your retirement with us here in Moscow, I'm thinking that you may have pressing business to tend to here that upped your timeline for this trip."

Gene kept a close look on the man's eyes searching for a clue as to his sincerity and meaning. This meeting was most impromptu, and it was beginning to seem like Nikolayevich really was looking to open a line of communication rather than seeking to gain information from him, or take him to some horrible hole for more extensive questioning. It was a most curious ordeal, for certain, he thought.

"I want to pass along how much we here in Russia are surprised about the attack you have suffered in your country," Nikolayevich said. "We in Russia understand very well how it is to be attacked by terrorists. We would like to offer any help we can to your government for getting to the bottom of this vicious act of war."

"That is very kind, Victor. Why are you telling me this? There are channels for this kind of thing, are there not? Channels other than retired tourists?"

Nikolayevich held out a card.

"My number, Mr. Davis. You can contact me anytime. I offer you my special number because, as I said, things are rarely as they seem."

"I see. Well, that is handy. Are you sure there's nothing you want to actually tell me, Victor? It seems like you might have more to say."

"Eugene, just let me just say this to you, you are welcome in Moscow now—I will keep an eye on you, but I will not interfere with your...[Nikolayevich paused rolling his eyes upwards as if looking for the correct word in English]...holiday."

Nikolayevich slapped the seat in front of him.

"The American Embassy," he said to the driver.

The car lurched forward into traffic, leaving the other men behind standing on the sidewalk.

"That's very kind, Victor," Gene said. "You guessed the destination of my walk, eh?"

"A lucky guess, indeed," he replied.

Chapter 31

Wickenburg Police Department
Wickenburg, Arizona
9:35 a.m.

Sherriff's detective Paul Jennings stood in front of half a dozen other local law enforcement officers in the briefing room.

"Detective Jennings will now fill us in on the shooting early this morning over at the Super 8," the Sherriff said after wrapping up a few other announcements.

"Well...it's a very sad deal, folks," the detective said. "Mrs. Nancy Miller was shot and killed early this morning. I knew her from church. A sweet young woman, only 24 years old, with a daughter and a husband Pete, who is a mechanic and drives that mobile tire repair truck here in town. She was running the desk on a midnight to eight shift. The circumstances surrounding this homicide are very strange. At about 5:00 a.m. a customer, a Mister Aleksandr Ivanovich Kuznetsov according to his credit card and room info, checked out at the front desk. Mrs. Miller was working the desk and was apparently the only one in the lobby at the time.

"We have footage from a surveillance camera that shows Kuznetsov check out at the counter and then walk across the lobby and sit down in a chair. The images aren't very good quality, but we can tell he is an older white male, approximately six feet tall, short gray hair, and wearing a dark suite. It looks like the only thing he had was a small shoulder bag and a small box of some kind that he was carrying."

Detective Jennings held up a large photograph of the suspect walking across the lobby taken from the surveillance video footage.

"We believe he must have been waiting on a ride—probably a cab. We are checking on the phone records, but we suspect it will show that Mrs. Miller likely called a cab for him. Don is following that lead and should have a line on what cab company so we can interview the driver if that is what happened.

"Five minutes later, this guy gets up out of his chair, walks towards the door—I'm guessing his cab just pulled up outside and he can see it through the glass doors—and he reaches under his suite coat, pulls out a pistol, and shoots Mrs. Miller twice in the chest. He never misses a beat, never slows his step, doesn't go to check if she was dead or alive...nothing. He just walks out cool as a cucumber. This is a cold blooded, deliberate, and heartless murder. His actions make it seem like a hit."

The detective paused for a moment, thinking about the victim. Grim looks occupied the faces of everyone in the room.

"So, no sign of robbery?" a uniformed officer asked. "He just got up, shot her, and walked out?"

"That's right," Jennings replied. "What the motivation could be for such a killing is still uncertain. It seems unlikely Mrs. Miller would be the target of a contract hit man, but we rule nothing out at this point and follow the evidence."

"Detective Jennings?" a young desk officer said.

"Yes, Mary?"

"I've been sending out a photo of a missing guy from the old folks home. He disappeared last night and it looks to me like he could be your guy."

"Let's have a look at that as soon as we wrap up here," the

detective said. "Any other questions?"

"Yes," another officer spoke up, "any idea what the weapon was?"

"We're waiting on the ballistics report," he replied, "but two bullets were recovered from the scene. They're a small caliber, consistent with a small pistol like the one seen in the video. Alright...that's what we know. I doubt this guy is still in town, but be aware just in case. Jones and Telling, you two come back with Mary and me and we'll see about this missing old guy. I might send you two over to whatever home he was in for a look around. Thanks, and all of you know to get in touch with me if you come across anything that might be related to this today."

Chapter 32

U. S. Embassy
Moscow, Russia
1:45 P. M.

"Gene Davis! You old coot!"

"John...it's good to see you, too," Gene replied. "Nice new place you've got here."

"American Embassy, Moscow...a guy could do worse. Come on in and have a seat."

"Well, actually John, I just lied to make you feel better," Gene said with a mischievous gleam in his eyes as he took a seat in front of the Ambassador's desk. "This massive weird rectangular block of a building with a metal grid thing stuck to the front... whatever-it-is...gives me a headache to look at. That embassy of yours in Tbilisi was a rectangle too, but at least there was some architectural merit to it."

The U. S. Ambassador to Russia, John Burrows, erupted into a hearty laugh.

"Gene, it is so refreshing to hear someone speak the blunt truth for a change!" John said. "That is rare in my line of work. And I'll be sure to let the President know how you feel about the look of this place."

"I think it's too late for an opinion to do much good, but feel free to pass along my thoughts," Gene said with a smile. "Last time we met I had you in my gun sights if I remember."

"Oh yes, that's right. You and your 'dakka, dakka, dakka' in my headset!" John exclaimed. "Which I assume you picked up from that classic 1969 Battle of Britain film where the commanding officer would take up a rookie and say 'attack, attack, attack,' in the headset when he was behind him pretending to shoot him, and it sounded more like 'dakka, dakka, dakka?' Nice touch, Gene—I love that film! Let's see, I was in the BF 109 that day and you were in a Spitfire, right?"

"Oh yes. A Spitfire Mk I and the 109 was an E-3, if I remember right—so a real Battle of Britain match up, eh?"

"Indeed, and you with that Spitfire...when you were on my six I tried to push into that dive and sucker you into taking negative Gs to see if the Spit's carburetor would stall you. That original Daimler-Benz 601 inverted V-12 engine in the 109 roared right along. What a plane!"

"I wasn't sure if that carburetor was original or not, but I wasn't going to chance following you down knowing your fuel injection would keep you humming and I might be dead in the air—so I pulled straight up, then into that Immelman looping over, and when you pulled out of the dive I got lucky and came right down behind you. A lag displacement roll and, 'dakka, dakka, dakka!'"

"I wouldn't call it luck, Ace," John said with a laugh. "That was a heck of move! Anyway, I've got a friend here who has some old Yaks I bet we could fly. He's just south of Moscow if you're going to be in town awhile? That's what retirement should be like, right—coming to Moscow to see an old friend and fly a few old warbirds?"

"Indeed! If only," Gene replied, shooting John a serious glance this time. "Your office secure?"

"Oh...you bet," John replied. "They tell me this place is tight. And here I thought you were just enjoying retirement, Gene."

Gene couldn't tell if John was kidding or not, but he was betting that was a joke.

"I was, two days ago...on my horse, gathering my cows on my own ranch under a ginormous Arizona sky. Paradise!"

"You've been talking about that for years. I'm surprised they suckered you back into this deal."

"Believe me, if D.C. didn't have a big fat hole in the middle of the beltway, I wouldn't be here."

"So what do you need?"

"First of all, you know this guy?"

Gene handed him Nikolayevich's card which only had the Russian's name and a telephone number printed on it in English letters.

"Victor Nikolayevich...never heard of him. I can get someone to look into him for you? What's he done?"

"He gave me a ride here from the hotel."

"Must be a heck of a nice guy then," John said, chuckling and studying Gene's face and awaiting his response.

"Indeed. If it hadn't been for the armed guys with him, getting boxed into the back of his Mercedes, and then him explaining how he was there to assist me, I might have thought what a splendid fellow for saving me a couple of block's walk. Not to mention he knew my name, that I had just retired, and knew when I arrived. I'm beginning to feel like a celebrity, which isn't a comforting feeling since I've made a living being a secret kind of agent for many decades now. I'm clearly no secret to anyone at this point."

"I'll see what I can come up with."

"Jeb dragged me into this, so let him know if you come up with anything and he can tell me. I'm not planning on being around Moscow long enough to hear about it."

"Well, air traffic is going to be messed up for awhile yet in the eastern half of the country since the second attack."

"Second attack? When?"

"This morning."

"How bad is it? What happened?"

"You hadn't heard? Where've you been, Pluto?"

"I've been in my hotel suite thinking...not watching the news or anything else."

"Retirement must be nice! Well, it was another missile. This one was shot down by our F-16s. Those birds have been on constant patrol over the capital since the first attack the other morning. That's all I know except that again there were no weapons of mass destruction involved and no reported serious damage this time."

Gene slipped a hand into his shirt pocket and withdrew the paper the waiter had delivered to his room.

"Jeb asked me to come here to Moscow and speak to some former acquaintances of mine and see if I could get a few more pieces of the puzzle about who pulled off the first attack."

"Well, if they flew you out of the States during the no-fly lockdown, I can see how high priority this is."

Gene handed the paper to John.

"I need you to pass along this bank account and routing info to Jeb. And that other number, the one with lots of zeros, that's the amount we need transferred—U.S. dollars. If you can send that over to him and let me know when the transfer is complete, then I can get back home to my horses and cows."

"No worries, Gene. I'll get right on this. Let's do it this way...if you don't hear from me within two hours, you're golden. If there's a snag, I'll call your cell and say, 'It was great seeing you today old buddy. If you've got time before you leave town, swing by again and we'll have dinner.'"

"That'll work. Thanks for the help, John. I'd love to take you up on the offer to fly those Yaks, but the next plane I'm getting on hopefully is taking me back towards home!"

Chapter 33

"Detective Jennings," the sheriff said, "this is state homicide detective, Bruce Lineman."

"Detective," Jennings responded, shaking his hand.

"With the strange nature of this case and the fugitive still on the run, I've called in help from the state boys. Can you fill him in on what you've got so far on the Miller murder?"

"Well, I'm guessing you're up to speed on the basics...she was shot to death, two shots to the chest, this morning at around 5:00 a.m. while working the front desk at the Super 8 Hotel on the edge of town. She died at the scene. We have surveillance footage of the murder."

"Yes, I read your initial report and have viewed that footage," Lineman said. "Anything new?"

"The guy in the video was registered at the hotel as...."

Jennings paused, pulled a small notebook from his shirt pocket, flipped it open, and found what he was looking for.

"Aleksandr Ivanovich Kuznetsov," he read aloud. "One of our officers recognized that he looked like an old fellow who went missing from a retirement home yesterday. From the hotel paperwork we know that this man had a working credit card and a New Mexico drivers license in the Russian name of Kuz-net-sov—that's a total tongue twister for me. Anyway, those documents check out as legit but the physical address used for both of them belongs to a family who has never heard of the guy—so that lead is bogus. And here's the thing, the guy who is missing from the retirement home, his name is Vassily Levin. Levin is a Russian who defected to the U.S. and became a citizen back in the 1960s. It would be a very strange coincidence for Wickenburg to have two old Russians running around matching this description. It's gotta be the same guy."

"What about his room at the retirement home?" Lineman asked.

"Nothing was missing as far as the nurses could tell, other than his laptop. The guy in the video has a shoulder bag that looks like it could be a laptop carrying bag. We went further back in the video footage from the hotel and found him checking in. It seems like he had no vehicle, no suitcase, no carry on bag like a traveler would. He just walked up to the place, so I'm convinced this is Levin. The staff at the home said he was a crotchety ol' cuss, but no one would have pegged him for a killer."

"How old is he?" Lineman asked.

"82. No previous record. Worked as a commercial pilot for most of his time here in the States and retired to Wickenburg a decade ago. He sold his house six months ago and has terminal cancer."

"That could be a stresser and it sent him off the deep end," Lineman said.

"So how does this old guy staying in an assisted living facility get ahold of a pistol and decide to go shoot an innocent person?" Jennings asked. "It just seems premeditated to me. We didn't find any connection between him and the Millers. I interviewed the victim's husband, Dave. He's just ripped apart about this, and has never heard of Levin or Kuz-net-zov, and says they don't know anybody at all with a Russian accent. And this is where it gets even weirder...preliminary findings from ballistics show that the bullets that killed Mrs. Miller, and the two spent casings found at the scene, were 9x18mm. The weapon was a Russian Makarov pistol—not the most obscure pistol in the world, but he didn't pick that up walking around Wickenburg for a couple of hours; it had to be his.

"The staff say there's no way he could have had it stashed in the home with him. I'm not so sure about that. Otherwise, there's only one gun shop in town. I already talked to the owner and our guy never went by there. Plus, he said there hasn't been a Makarov in that shop in years. If you didn't know better, you'd think this was some kind of Russian mob hit, except that we're in Wickenburg, Arizona. And, I can tell you, Mrs. Miller was just a mother and wife working the late shift to help make ends meet for her family. No one in the family has a prior record other than a speeding ticket the husband got two years ago. We're looking into them, but I can tell you they're going to turn out clean."

"Any word on the shooter's getaway?" Lineman asked.

"Mrs. Miller called him a cab," Jennings continued. "I interviewed the driver myself. He said the customer was an old man with a strong Russian accent, but that his English was quite good. He didn't get a name, and the man paid in cash with a hefty tip. I checked the serial numbers on the bills—they're fairly recent and there's nothing out of the ordinary with them. The cab driver had the guy pegged as a businessman from out of town who was just in Wickenburg for a day and got caught in the air traffic shut down yesterday from the attack on D.C. He dropped the suspect off at the American Airlines departure terminal at the airport in Phoenix. He said the guy mentioned returning to L.A., and since air traffic had resumed to the western half of the country, he didn't think anything was out of the ordinary."

"Clearly the cabby didn't hear the shots?" Lineman asked

rhetorically.

"Nope," Jennings confirmed.

"I guess it's time to contact the airlines about departing passenger names at that time to see if we get lucky with Levin or Kuznetsov. And, dig through video footage from the airport," Lineman said, looking less than enthusiastic about the prospect of the latter task.

"He got dropped off at about 7:30 a.m.," Jennings added. "So at least you've got a time and that right terminal entrance to narrow down that video search."

Chapter 34

Sheremetyevo International Airport
Moscow, Russia
5:11 p.m.

Gene entered the Moscow airport, waded through security, and took a seat near his departure gate just outside of a Burger King.

"A Burger King in Moscow," Gene thought to himself. The disbelief still abounded in his mind and spoke to how his reality of Russia remained from a much different era. He had heard McDonald's had managed to open stores in the Soviet Union in 1990, but he had not seen any of them himself. The uniquely American and completely capitalist franchise before him was a bit of a jolt to his antiquated senses that kept expecting the latitude and longitude where he sat to be devoid of such enterprises. It seemed Moscow was like anywhere in the west these days.

Honestly, when he considered the changes all around him from what he had known of Russia before, it made him think that other parts of the world really were not immune from sweeping, unthinkable, and rather sudden changes either. That put a little fear in him when he considered the recent attacks on Washington, D.C.

Gene's thoughts shifted to the task at hand. A couple of hours remained before his flight was scheduled to board. The contact from Anna should be meeting him at any time now. He envisioned some random fellow, like the waiter from the hotel, coming along and sitting two seats over from him who would read a newspaper for a few minutes. Then he would fold the paper, set it on the seat between them, get up and leave, and the paper would contain his message—old school spycraft in action.

He couldn't have been more wrong.

Anna stood out like a beacon a block away walking towards him through the sea of generic travelers. It was a shock, though he tried to play it cool when the tall, slender woman sauntered up in a fire-engine-red coat that fit her tightly and to a tee from the waist up, with long lapels, two big black buttons, and a hood which she wore over her head, and which from the waist down flared out into a skirt-like arrangement that swayed with the motion of her body and stopped at her knees. Black fur accented the garment, trimming the bottom edge of the skirt, her cuffs, and her hood through which her angular face appeared with two curiously colored eyes beaming out. The whole look was set off by black soft suede leather knee-high boots with high heels.

Gene overcame a momentary paralysis at the sight of her and then managed to stand as she approached. Aglaya stopped before him, holding her hands together at her waist and unconsciously, and girlishly, twisted slightly from side-to-side causing the bottom half of the coat to swish playfully back and forth around her thighs.

Gene simply couldn't manage to speak a greeting at first as she stood before him looking radiant and anything but incognito. In fact, he was very aware of scores of passers-by in the place checking out the striking presence of this elegant woman in the terminal, and he wouldn't have been the least bit surprised if there had been a huge pile-up of pedestrian traffic before they were finished meeting.

"Hello, cowboy!"

"Well, howdy ma'am," Gene finally managed to utter, playing it up, and tipping his cowboy hat to her. "Are you traveling?"

"I am. And, fancy meeting you here!"

Gene was about to take her hand in greeting when she just spread her arms wide, moved in, embraced him in a full-on hug, and he found himself kissing her on the lips.

"Gadzooks!" was all Gene could manage to say when she released him.

Aglaya smiled wide and gazed at him with those grulla colored eyes.

"My, what big eyes you have!" Gene said, making a Little Red Riding Hood allusion, which he honestly thought might be a closer analogy than he cared to consider.

Aglaya swished more animatedly and chuckled.

Gene smiled back at her, though with a completely deer-in-the-headlights look on his face.

"This is for you," she said, handing Gene a wrapped package about the size of a large mug. "Don't open it yet, darling. Wait until you are on the plane and then think of me as you fly away."

"Thank you, Aglaya," he said. "I certainly will."

She pulled him in and hugged him tightly again, this time her lips brushed lightly against his right ear. He heard her slight breath, then she whispered softly:

"Gene, this 'present' should answer some of your questions. What I discovered is that some of our most secret sleeper agents' information from the old Soviet days has been sold to the highest bidder. These are remarkably old, deep cover sleepers who were never decommissioned, so old that many may be dead by now. In one lot, 20 operatives in the west including America have had their activation information sold to Muslim extremists. I'm not sure who the buyer was, but I hope to find out."

Anna stiffened her grip on him.

"I was able to purchase only what is in the box for you," she said. "But oh, the seller was delighted to be paid double for something he had already cashed in on! It makes me sick how no one has any loyalty anymore. Traitors! No beliefs beyond profit... no...no desire to create a better world beyond one's own greed. Our country, our revolution, our industry...the sacrifice was great. The things we achieved! And now it is just a rummage sale around here."

Anna paused. Gene felt her chest heave as she drew in a few deep breaths. The two still hugged one another tightly.

"Look at me," she whispered, "I now have more in common with my old enemy than my new countrymen. Anyway, Gene, you should know that our old agents are true to their country and their missions. They know not what they do. These well funded terrorist brutes who would use them this way...you find them and you drive a stake through their wicked hearts."

The tall, slender woman softened. Gene held her tightly a moment more, kissed her on the cheek, and then released the embrace.

"You're a gem Aglaya Bobrova...a real gem. And I will, but you realize I have to go after the agents."

Aglaya's eyes, peering from under her hood through the black fur, changed from fiery to sad in an instant as they remained fixed on his own.

"Yes, Gene," she whispered. "I know this."

Chapter 35

I-40, Eastbound
7:21 p.m.

Vassily was eager to reach his destination but knew he should avoid any chance of being pulled over by the police for speeding. The car had cruise control, and he kept it dialed-in at about three miles over the speed limit for good measure as he charged forward east along Interstate 40. He left Arizona, entered and exited New Mexico, blew through the thin top part of Texas, and then entered Oklahoma.

He had been driving for 11 hours, and fatigue was setting in. For the first time since he left the home, the pain began to creep back into his body and reminded him of his cancerous condition.

A road sign said Oklahoma City was 30 miles ahead. Vassily did not feel like taking on the traffic of a large city before resting. He took the next exit off the Interstate, a town called El Reno.

When he got off the exit, he drove a short distance and saw a hotel. He pulled in, parked, and thought through his next few steps: rest, food (not necessarily in that order), then again on towards his first objective. He could check in and get his room, then run out for dinner...or better yet, just have a pizza delivered—the town surely seemed large enough to have a pizza delivery service—then grab some sleep. He should easily make the objective by lunch time the next day and be right on schedule.

Now that he was activated, he needed to tune into the shortwave broadcasts once in every 24 hour period to see if there were any additional messages for him. That would mean another early morning awakening to tune in the shortwave.

Chapter 36

Gene sat in a window seat on a Finnair Airbus A330-300 in front of the wing. He enjoyed the unobstructed view of the twinkling heavens and the dark sea below. He felt lucky to have gotten his preferred seat on such a short notice. The flight from Moscow to Helsinki had been smooth. With air traffic now resumed over the United States with the exception of Washington, D.C. airspace, extra flights at odd hours had been arranged by Finnair to accommodate the backlog of passengers trying to get from Europe to the United States. So without time to sit for a moment he had deplaned and replaned in Helsinki and was on a rare night flight from Helsinki to New York.

Gene wasn't sure how Anna had gotten a wrapped "present" past the security of Moscow's Sheremetyevo International Airport, but the woman certainly was a pro, and very well connected, so he figured he shouldn't be surprised. Now that he was over the Atlantic Ocean in the middle of the night, and the passengers beside him were asleep in their seats, he reached into his small computer bag that was stashed under the seat in front of him and retrieved the mug-sized present. He removed a blue bow and then quietly unfolded the fancy wrapping paper that was covered with a green, yellow, and red flower pattern. He popped open the top of the box which revealed a typical Russian *matryoshka* doll. The edges of his mouth bent upwards into a smile as he removed the toy.

"Well now, *babushka*," Gene said aloud softly, which was Russian for grandmother—his reference was both to the look of the female figure painted on the doll and to how this type of doll is commonly called a *babushka* doll, "what secrets do you hold for me?"

Gene twisted the top from the bottom of the doll which split it in half. He removed the upper half revealing another smaller doll within the first one. He took out the next one and twisted her open which revealed yet another smaller doll inside, and so on. He couldn't help but chuckle at Anna's playful method of conveying such secret information, and he was wondering what exactly could be in the last doll and how small it would be.

By the fifth doll, they were getting pretty tiny. Doll tops and bottoms were covering his lap precariously. The final little egg of a doll was painted up to be a baby and it was made from a solid piece of wood.

"Hmmm," he thought. "Nice present, Anna. But what does baby *babushka* here have to tell me."

The small, solid doll was about the size of a peanut. He tried twisting it a couple of times, but no, it was not going to split in two. Gene reached into his computer bag and fumbled around until he laid his hands on a glasses case. Inside were a pair of strong reading glasses. He put them on and had a closer look.

The doll seemed solid, sure enough. Gene turned it upside down and saw a tiny slot cut into the wood on the bottom. Putting a thumbnail into the slot, he tried to twist to see if the bottom might unscrew. He had no luck. He slipped a hand into his pocket and pulled out a dime. The edge of the dime fit into the slot nicely and with the extra leverage, the bottom broke loose and began to spin. It unscrewed and revealed a small compartment drilled up into the center of the tiny doll.

Gene held the doll in one hand and shook it hard into the other. A rolled up tiny pad of papers shot out onto his palm.

"Jumpin' jemminy crickets!" he thought. "Now we're getting somewhere."

Gene peered out of the corner of his eye to the passengers sitting to his right. The closest was an older woman, her head tilted back at what seemed like a painful angle. Her eyes were closed and her mouth was open. She had to be unconscious to be in that position, he surmised. The next seat over was occupied by a man who had his arms crossed, his head was bowed down, and he was snoring.

Gene put *babushka* back together, except for the baby doll which he kept separate. He released and lowered the small table that was hinged on the back of the seat in front of him. He set the tiny scroll onto the hard plastic surface and attempted to smooth it out flat. It didn't work very well, so he took the papers and counter-bent them with his fingers managing to get them pretty straight. The scroll was a very small tablet with one edge of the papers fastened together with a rubber-like substance. Gene brought the tiny pad up towards his nose and with his reading glasses, the writing on the top sheet came into clear focus.

"Holy smokes!" he said aloud but quietly. "Can it be?"

Gene looked to his right relieved to see his sudden outburst had not disturbed his sleeping neighbors.

He carefully flipped through to other pages of the tiny tablet. Each sheet of paper was covered in columns of numbers, each five digits wide. This was a one-time pad, and an old one at that.

"Could it be?" Gene wondered again.

He reached down and shuffled around in his bag and pulled out the sheets of paper Jeb had given him with the messages from The English Man.

"There's no way," he thought. "The odds are against it, but what if...?"

Chapter 37

State Police Headquarters
Phoenix, Arizona
7:30 a.m.

State homicide detective Lineman had ridden out with sheriff's detective Jennings and looked around the crime scene for himself. He had found nothing there to add any insights into what he already had learned about the case. Then, he had headed back to Phoenix to his office.

"Hey Bruce," an officer at the front desk said when he entered the building. "This came in for you. It's the surveillance footage from Sky Harbor Airport."

Lineman swung by the desk and the officer handed him an envelope.

"You know," he said, "on TV, detectives always have these incredibly clever geeks that do this looking-through-footage stuff for them. They 'enhance' images with some secret software or have fancy 'face recognition software.' How is it that I always get stuck looking at hours of cruddy video myself with no fancy anything, eh?"

"Hollywood has a much bigger budget than we do, you know," the officer shot back at him.

"Well, there is that!" Lineman replied and laughed as he headed down the hall that led to his office.

He plugged the flash drive into his computer and began viewing the video files that showed throngs of people entering the departure terminal at the doors closest to the American Airlines counter. He started five minutes before the time the cab driver said he dropped the man off hoping that it wouldn't take long to find the guy he was looking for.

Luck was on Lineman's side. Almost immediately he spotted an older man in a suit with a bag over his shoulder carrying something under one arm enter through the doors. This traveler both met the description of the shooter and matched the man he had seen in the surveillance footage from the hotel shooting. But rather than go to a departure check-in counter or automated airline check-in machine, the man walked briskly straight down the terminal and out of view of the camera. The detective made a few clicks of his mouse and brought up a different camera angle taken at the same time and likewise found the old man walking down the terminal. The man passed out of view again.

Lineman repeated the drill and picked the old man up on yet a third camera angle. This time, he watched as the man descended an escalator to a lower section of the airport that was for arrivals and baggage claim. He didn't have video footage from that part of the airport, so he picked up the phone and called Sky Harbor Airport's security to get them to prepare it for him.

Chapter 38

Rural Arkansas
10:05 a.m.

Vassily drove along the weathered gray pavement of state route 364 near Wynne, Arkansas. The road was arrow straight with wide gravel shoulders that dropped suddenly into sharp ditches on either side. White lines marked the edges of the pavement and the broken yellow line running down the center of the road was barely visible due to a streak of yellowish brown asphalt that had been laid along the middle of the road as a patch before the last line painting had been done.

Large flat fields came right up to the ditches on both sides of the road, and the old man could see trees off in the distance at the far ends of the fields. The crops all had been harvested recently—most likely soybeans, he guessed. The stubble remained with interesting wavy tracks all around made by the tires of the harvesting equipment.

Vassily had seen an abundance of fields like these over the years, but from the perspective of a pilot flying over them. That overhead vantage point gave a much larger impression, one like a giant patchwork quilt laid out on the earth below him. In the fall, he would look down upon the large combines at work as the darker green or yellow rectangles diminished and were replaced by the lighter colored stubble. It seemed like the machines made ever-larger light colored frames along the edges of the fields which grew until entire fields were one color again. It was a sight he recalled from his younger years, too, back home in his mother country flying over vast farmlands as he trained and worked as a fighter pilot.

Vassily squinted as he looked for the next house and mailbox on the right side of the road. With only one or two houses and the occasional church every so many miles the task was not difficult. It was made easier because any structures usually were surrounded by big trees in the otherwise empty, flat farmland, and thus they stood out like skyscrapers in a sandbox.

Finally, he approached a farm on the right that had a ranch house close to the road, plenty of large trees in the yard, and many barns and other metal buildings arranged neatly behind it. The green mailbox had "716" painted on the side in black. This was the place.

His heart began to race.

Vassily pulled the rental car into the driveway and stopped close to the house. He got out and knocked on the door. He could feel his pulse throbbing in his neck and wrists—it was the feeling he used to get when flying into combat.

How would this go, he wondered? Surely the agent also had received his activation messages from the numbers station and knew he would be arriving. But what would he say if things didn't go well? What if....

"Hello," an old man said, opening a storm door and looking at Vassily.

"Hallo," Vassily greeted him in return.

Vassily at least was reassured that the man he was facing was about his age. He paused for another second, his mind racing.

"Can I help you?" the man asked in a perfect mid-western American accent, shifting a little from side to side as he stood.

Vassily was struck dumb for a few moments but then

managed to croak out, "Butterfly."

The moment between them seemed to be frozen in time; seconds crept by like minutes. Finally, the man who had answered the door shifted his weight again.

"Butterfly?" he asked. "Oh yes, well, butterfly."

"Da," Vassily replied, smiling. "Butterfly."

"Uh, okay. Just give me a moment."

The man disappeared into the house and then returned wearing a jacket. He stepped outside with Vassily.

"Follow me in your car."

"Okay," Vassily said.

Vassily had imagined this moment many times in his life. It wasn't anything like how he had thought it would be. He assumed he and any of his contacts would be kindred spirits. He thought the camaraderie would be palpable like it had been between him and the other pilots back in the Soviet Air Force. He expected a special connection with one who had spent a long lifetime of hiding a huge secret and then finally seeing the success of it about to be unleashed.

Instead, it felt like he was visiting a total stranger. And not just a stranger, but one who really wanted to get rid of him as quickly as possible. Of course they were secret agents, so it had to be different from his pilot comrades...but still, they were working for the same cause. The cold distance between them at this important moment surprised him.

The man got into an old 1970s Ford F-150 pickup truck with a flat bed, started it, and began driving down the farm road beyond his house. Vassily trailed in the dust behind him in his rental car.

They drove about half a mile and came to another cluster of farm buildings, this one with metal grain silos and two old concrete silos with metal dome roofs. The man parked his pickup right by one of the towering concrete silos and climbed out of the truck. Vassily parked beside him and got out of the car.

"Follow me," the man said.

They walked into a small building at the base of a silo where a chute went through the roof and up to the top of the silo accessible from inside the building. They walked over to it. A hopper that fed a conveyor belt arrangement was positioned just below the chute. Vassily twisted himself to get a look up the chute and could see wooden doors in place every few feet up the length of the silo inside the chute. He had never been close to a silo before, but it seemed obvious that the doors were there to block the silage inside the silo when it was filled. It seemed they were removed from the top down as the level of the silage lowered to be able to continue to unload silage into the chute.

"Over here," the man said.

They walked about a quarter of the way around the base of the silo. The man moved a pile of old feed bags and some other defunct equipment in the corner of the building out of the way revealing an obscure door, about half the size of a normal door, built into the base of the silo. Reaching into his jacket pocket, the man pulled out a key. It fit into a lock on the door. He turned it and the door swung outward and opened.

The opening revealed a dark space leading under the silo. The man felt around inside the doorway, flipped a switch, and a light came on.

"I'll get what you need," he said, sitting down on the ground and then sliding through the doorway.

Vassily knelt down and peered into the room. It was directly beneath the silo, was round, and was the circumference of the silo. He was surprised at how clean things looked inside the bunker-like space, and that there seemed to be no dank smell coming from it. There were several sets of metal shelves inside full of boxes of various sizes.

The man came back and handed a large back pack up to

Vassily through the door.

"Here you go," he said.

Vassily grabbed it by the straps. He remembered from his training that it weighed 55 pounds. His diminished strength was evident when he only managed to drag the back pack through the door and across the concrete floor far enough to be out of the way.

The man disappeared into the room again. When he returned, he was carrying a bag case about the size of a briefcase and a rifle that Vassily easily recognized as an AK-47 of sorts, but this one was so stubby he knew he had never seen its type before. The man handed those things up to Vassily and then climbed out through the door.

"So, just to refresh your memory," the man said, "this back pack holds the RA-115. It has been here plugged into grid power. I just disconnected it and the battery is full, so you have several weeks of time for the device to be in fine shape before you'd need to worry about plugging it in again. I'm guessing that's more than enough time for you to complete your mission."

"Yes, it is," Vassily said.

Vassily looked at the device closely. It was a time-capsule to those days long ago when he had trained for this mission before leaving Russia.

"Here are a few grenades, just in case," the man said. "And the AK is, well, an AK, just because you never know."

"It's very short," Vassily commented.

"Yes she is," the man replied. "This is an *Okurok*."

Vassily laughed.

"A cigarette stub; I can see zat," he commented.

"Officially she is an AKS74U," the man replied. "There are a few extra 30 round clips for it in the bag. Just so you know, it shoots 5.45 x 39 millimeter rounds, not the standard AK 7.62 x 39 round."

The other man was easily the stronger of the two and he picked up and carried the backpack with no problem; Vassily carried the bag and the rifle. Not a word passed between them as they loaded all of the gear into the trunk of the rental car. Vassily was half the reason nothing more was said, but he really had no desire to speak. He assumed it was the same for the other fellow.

Once everything was loaded up, Vassily opened the car door to get behind the wheel, but he took one last look at the other man before he got in.

The man looked back at him. He had no expression at all.

"Comrade," Vassily said.

"Comrade," the man replied.

Vassily slipped in behind the wheel, started the car, and headed back down the farm road on his way.

Chapter 39

Gene knew he only needed to work on the first line or two of each message to reveal if anything relatively intelligible was being deciphered. Honestly, it would be so rare for a numbers station message to make any sense that it would stand out to him "like a bull in a bakery," he thought to himself. He chuckled at his own joke enjoying it way too much, a sure sign that he was getting tired.

Even with the pad from Anna, deciphering any of the messages was a long shot at best. Was it the right pad? Was the top page the correct page for a given message? What language was being used? The list went on. Heck, modern computers and a team of cryptologists at Langley could have their work cut out for them even with the right pad if the other factors of how the messages were coded remained unknown.

Still, he knew the typical methods for coding messages with a one-time pad. He decided to try the most obvious possibilities first to cross them off the list. Besides, he was fascinated by the numbers station messages, and he certainly didn't have anything better to do while flying over the ocean for the next several hours.

He got a pencil and got to work.

Two hours later Gene had deciphered nothing but nonsense.

He was used to that when spending time with numbers station numbers. Honestly, he had never minded scribbling away at this task since the numbers always held the promise of gold. No, it was even more than that. He knew for a fact that he was holding golden nuggets of intelligence right there in his hands; he just needed to pan them out somehow. It was easy for him to see how a guy could head for the hills and spend all week panning in a creek for gold. He reminded himself to never start gambling.

Gene was down to the second to the last message. He was trying the English alphabet with the most basic 26 letter/10 numeral arrangement. He wrote down the first 20 digits from the next message on the notebook on which he was scratching figures, then placed the first 20 digits from the top sheet of the one-time pad from Anna under them. Reversing the modular addition he got a line of numbers: 09030 50215 24010 32009. He separated them into pairs: 09 03 05 02 15 24 01 03 20 09

He began assigning English letters: I, C, E....

"Hmmm," he hummed quietly, a little surprised that from all the many attempts at deciphering a message so far no three random letters had spelled any word.

He continued: B, O, X, A, C, T, I.

The hair stood up all over his arms and legs as little electrical shocks of excitement snapped him to being more fully awake than he had felt in hours. In all of his years of tracking number station transmissions, this was the very first time he had a decipher pad in his possession that seemed to work.

Gene worked furiously, scribbling frantically to get the full message. With it finished he carefully studied the results and was astonished at how much information it contained. Obviously the Soviets had been unconcerned about the one-time pad being deciphered. Or if what Anna had said was true and the mission now was being instigated by someone else, perhaps it required taking a chance to extend extra information to the agents in the field quickly. Whatever the reason, he was about to bust with the need to get off that plane and get this intelligence to Jeb immediately.

He took a couple of deep breaths and read over the decoded message again. It said:

ICEBOX ACTIVE PROCEED TO CACHE 54 PROCURE RA115 CONTACT IS 037 CODEWORD BUTTERFLY THEN PROCEED TO FLUSHING 26 OCT 1200 TARGET WALL STREET

Chapter 40

EOD Mobile Unit
Arlington, Virginia
3:14 a.m.

"McAbee," Master Chief McAbee grumbled into the cell phone that had just woken him with the sound of several bursts from a 50 caliber machine gun, his ring-tone of choice.

"Master Chief," the petty officer said tentatively into the cell phone, "you said you would like to be updated immediately if anything 'notable' happened."

"That's right, Petty Officer...so out with it, son."

"Right, well, we've been monitoring the major news outlets and in the past two minutes they've gotten the story, Master Chief."

"What do mean, exactly?"

"Someone has leaked the video taken by those students of the first incoming missile and it's all over the television and online. It's the middle of the night but already they've made the connection that this was no scud, and that it looks a lot like a V-1. They're going nuts with it already."

McAbee laughed.

"Oh boy, the White House is going to be busy today," McAbee said, more to himself than to the petty officer. "Thanks for the heads-up on this. Make sure there's fresh coffee on—I'm coming on in now to see how this rodeo goes."

Chapter 41

State Police Headquarters
Phoenix, Arizona
10:10 p.m.

Detective Lineman went into an office where a secure video conference was being set up via computer with the FBI. Apparently he was not the only who worked late, he thought.

"Have a seat," the computer tech said, not looking at the detective but rather keeping his eyes glued to the computer in front of him.

Lineman sat down in a chair in front of a computer screen at a desk beside the tech.

"Man, you've got nice chairs in here," Lineman said.

The tech kept punching keys on his computer and ignored the remark.

"It's okay, man," Lineman continued, "no need to feel guilty."

The tech continued ignoring him.

"Oh, and that's a nice laptop!" Lineman said.

The detective stood up quickly, shuffled over to another table, and haphazardly opened up the object of his interest.

"Boy, I could use one of these," he said.

"Don't touch that!" the tech blurted out.

Lineman gave him a stern look and said:

"That's, 'don't touch that, *detective.*'"

Lineman kept himself between the laptop and the tech so the fellow could not get a look at what he was doing. He pretended to slap some keys.

"Please don't touch that, *detective*!" the tech blurted out with duress clearly in his voice.

Lineman chuckled and slapped the laptop shut with a sharp clap.

"No worries, man," Lineman said, noticing the tech was now looking at him, at least. "But I think I'm going to request a transfer over here to your department...just for this chair if nothing else."

Lineman sat back down in his proper place. The tech, looked relieved like a parent who just got his two-year-old to sleep. He turned back to his computer. With a couple of mouse clicks, the live feed to the FBI popped up on the screen in front of the detective.

"Detective Lineman," said a woman who appeared on the screen, "I'm agent Lopez. What have you got for me?"

"Nice to meet you, agent," Lineman said slowly, deliberately, and overly nice as a slight stall—a knee-jerk reaction for him to the direct way Lopez was diving right into business.

He paused just long enough draw that moment out a bit further to see if she would jump in and hustle him along or if she could hold it together and wait for him to continue. He pegged her as being in her early 30s, ambitious, and all about the job. He was a detective after all, and could not help but detect things about people, even in this scenario.

She remained perfectly stoic, not taking the bait. Lineman grinned at her approvingly.

"We were briefed this morning on your unusual call to state police departments across the country to report any strange activity involving Russian nationals," Lineman began. "Well, I've got a doozie for you. A murder suspect on the run. I was going to pass this one over to you guys today anyway since he's apparently fled over state lines. But, since you're looking for 'Russian' and 'strange' I contacted you straight away. So what's with the interest in Russians, anyway?"

"What details can you provide on the case?" Lopez replied, curtly.

Lineman just sat there, pausing uncomfortably long this time, just looking at the agent.

"Just going to avoid my question altogether?" Lineman finally broke the quiet standoff.

"Detective Lineman," Lopez said in a way that reminded Lineman of his sixth grade teacher, Mrs. Snellingsworth, "we have on ongoing investigation and I can not discuss any details of it, except to say that there is possibly a Russian connection and we're just trying to connect some dots and get a lucky break. So if you don't mind, out with the details of your case so I can either run with it or pass it along to the proper department."

"Must be something big then, given such high priority and getting such an energetic agent as yourself on point," Lineman replied.

He paused again, just for effect.

Lopez just looked at him unblinkingly.

"Okay," Lineman continued, finally, "this case may be what you're looking for; it's that weird. We have an 82-year-old Russian who went AWOL from a retirement home in Wickenburg, Arizona. Somehow the guy comes up with a fake I.D. and credit card, and a Makarov pistol, stays the night in a hotel, gets up super early, checks out, has the young woman at the desk call him a cab, and we have him on security camera footage getting up from a chair in the lobby, walking out the door, and shooting her twice in the chest as he walks past her."

Lineman thought Lopez's eyes brightened up, but he was not sure.

"It's one of the most random, deliberate, and cold-hearted things I've ever seen," he added, "and I've seen plenty in my time in homicide. The rest of the details I think will greatly interest you, as well, Miss Lopez."

Lineman paused again...and waited wondering if the "miss" would strike any reaction, but she took it like a pro and it just rolled right off her back. He cleared his throat, paused a little longer, and watched the agent's face. She was a cool customer. He would hate to interrogate her, he thought, but he knew she had to be squirming with at least a little anticipation.

"So...here's the thing," Lineman continued. "We know the fella somehow came from Russia back in the 1960s when that sort of thing just didn't happen. He had to have defected somehow. His name is Vassily Levin...at least that's been his name since becoming a U.S. citizen. The name on his documents from the hotel, however, was Aleksandr Ivanovich Kuznetsov. All this is in the file that is being e-mailed to you by my friend over there at that very, very nice computer of his."

The tech just kept looking straight ahead at his computer stroking keys.

Lineman paused again, deliberately.

"Right, so our Russian suspect shoots the young woman—a Mrs. Miller—exits the lobby, gets into a cab, and off he goes. Local police interviewed the cabby who took the man to the airport in Phoenix, that's Sky Harbor Airport. The guy paid cash with a hefty tip and told the cabby he was flying back to L.A. Instead, however, I viewed the security camera footage from the airport...by the way, Lopez, do you have people that do that sort of thing for you?"

Lineman paused.

"What?" the agent asked, frowning and shaking her head slightly this time.

"You know, watching hours of security camera footage. Do

you have people there who do that for you, with fancy face recognition software to make it super fast and all that?"

"It depends," Lopez answered. "But the case, Detective Lineman, let's see if we can keep you focused on the case, shall we?"

"Right," he said, reminded again of old Mrs. Snellingsworth.

Lineman paused and pretended to be re-collecting his thoughts. He enjoyed that she was starting to crack around the edges, and he bet she never had to look through video footage, ever.

"So, I watched all this video from the airport *myself*, all these zillion different angles, and discovered that rather than check in for a flight to L.A., he just walked through the departure terminal, went down the escalator to the lower level, went to baggage claim, and there he exited the building and took a shuttle bus to the rental car place which is a few miles away in its own massive building. So then I had to get the video footage from that place and sift through it."

Lineman paused awhile, finally fake coughed, and rolled his head as if his neck was stiff and bugging him.

Lopez just sat there stoically, not biting this time.

"Right," Lineman continued, "so he rents a car. I went over and interviewed the folks at the rental place he used, and guess what?"

This time it was Lopez who paused, just waiting for the answer.

"No guess?" Lineman asked.

Lopez just sat there staring at him blankly on the screen.

"Well, I'll tell you," the detective began again, "he rented the car under yet another name complete with a valid driver's license and credit card. This time under the name, Steven Harper. Steven Harper...can you believe this guy? That's the most un-Russian name ever, right? And the license and credit card aren't stolen, they're legit, so this is really weird.

"The guy is 82, in a retirement home dying from cancer...did I mention the cancer part? He has like a few months to live, and then suddenly he slips out of the home on foot, gets his hands on a Makarov and a bunch of valid I.D.s and credit cards, and he was born in Soviet Russia. I may not be a genius, Lopez, but even I can see where this is heading. And with that massive crater right outside the Pentagon, I have to say I'm not thinking happy thoughts here."

"So what's the latest?" Lopez asked, breaking her silence.

"We have the description of the rental car and the license plate—that's in the info coming your way—and we already have an APB out on him here in Arizona. But I'm guessing he drove straight out of state to somewhere else."

"Does the rental car have a tracker?" Lopez asked.

"Nope. It's a budget outfit. He actually got a heck of a deal on the rental—excellent senior discount. I was impressed."

Lopez paused.

"Detective Lineman," she said.

"Yes, Agent Lopez," he replied.

"This is very helpful information," she said. "I greatly appreciate you getting it to us right away and for taking our request for information seriously. Will you let me know straight away if you come across anything else?"

"Of course," Lineman replied, earnestly. "With what this guy did to that poor woman, a wife with kids, I'll do anything to help you find him."

Chapter 42

Westbound over the Atlantic Ocean
Wee Hours of the Morning

Gene, having been a CIA agent for the latter part of the Cold War, and with a vast smorgasbord of military information stored in his head, actually knew that the RA 115 was a suitcase nuke. The thought caused him to reflect on the recent V-1 attacks. Those missiles were much too big for a guy to just pick up from a cache and take somewhere easily. But by contrast, the suitcase nuke was small enough for a man to pack around fairly easily. That, along with the situation in Washington, D.C. proving whoever was behind this was willing to go through with attacks, had him extremely concerned.

The message clearly defined the target as Wall Street, which meant New York City. The message's mention of "FLUSHING" gave Gene an instant twinge of urgency because he realized he had a pretty good idea of what that meant. Not many people knew about it anymore, but he bet that the reference was to Flushing Airfield. Being an aircraft buff from way back, Gene knew quite a bit about the abandoned airfield. In fact, he even had climbed the perimeter fence and walked around the place about 20 years ago, unable to resist the temptation to go in and see what remained of the once thriving airport.

He remembered that Flushing Airfield had opened in Queens,

New York in 1927—that was just the kind of fact that stuck in his mind. He had been fascinated to learn that during its first decade of operation the airport had been the busiest in New York. By 1939, it was losing ground to LaGuardia, but it remained open over the years. Gene remembered that in the 1960s the Goodyear blimp had been based there. The airport finally closed in 1984.

Gene realized now that Flushing Airfield was the perfect place to get an aircraft close to downtown New York City if someone wanted to launch an attack of some kind. His hike into the abandoned property revealed acres of overgrown land concealing the still serviceable hard-top runway which was positioned to the interior of the property. A high chain link fence stood century around the perimeter of the whole area cutting it off, more or less, from the surrounding population. Even two decades after closing its gates the paved runways had been in decent shape. Gene bet they remained usable, at least for a small plane.

A smaller aircraft could swoop right down and land completely out of sight of anyone around on the ground. Someone might notice a plane coming in for a landing, but once on the ground, there would be no way for anyone to see what was going on and there would be plenty of time for a secret rendezvous with someone before taking off again.

Downtown Manhattan was only about a 20 minute drive from Flushing Airfield, and that drive included making a big curve along Interstate 495. A plane could fly a direct path to the heart of New York City in a matter of minutes from Flushing. LaGuardia was right between Flushing and Manhattan, but if the aircraft did not have a transponder to squawk a code to the tower there, it might easily fly right past the busy airport with no one noticing that plane as being out of the ordinary until it was too late. It also would be a perfect place to launch a drone. He had been thinking old school due to the V-1s, the old one-time-pad, and Anna's intelligence, but there was no reason not to consider that this might be, at least in part, a modern high tech attack in the making.

Of course, this was just a hunch, but Gene's gut told him it was right. That gut of his felt like it had when he was about to go into combat back in Vietnam, and it had served him well there.

If he was right about all this, then he was probably right about the last part of the message—and that really had him feeling trapped in his seat. "12 Oct" was today. "1200" had to be the time, but was that local time or Greenwich Mean Time? If it was local time, he barely had enough time to get on the ground and call Jeb to alert him.

Gene would do that, but getting various authorities to respond took time. There might be no time to foil the attack. His brain began to buzz with what he might be able to do to stop it.

Chapter 43

FBI Headquarters
Washington, D.C.
4:30 a.m.

FBI Agent Cecelia Lopez couldn't sleep. She had dozed off by 11:00 p.m., but at 2:17 a.m., according to the cell phone she checked beside the bed, her brain had snapped awake. Despite an effort to get more sleep by burying her head beneath a pillow, her mind quickly shifted into high gear. She relentlessly churned over various ways to hunt down the old Russian murderer from Arizona. Finally, she gave up trying to go back to sleep, got dressed, made coffee, and headed in to her office at FBI headquarters on Pennsylvania Avenue to get busy finding the fugitive.

Commuting into Washington, D. C. remained a round-about undertaking for Lopez since her regular route still was blocked by the blast zone from the first missile. At 4:00 a.m. the detour north was nearly devoid of traffic. She thought it might be worth loosing sleep more often if it cut an hour off of her drive to work.

Lopez had wrapped up her video call with Detective Lineman the previous day and immediately set the ball rolling to put all the resources of the FBI that were at her disposal into action to apprehend the old Russian suspect. Lineman had been correct in his clever assumptions connecting FBI interest in Russian nationals to the terrorist attacks. But Lopez likewise was trying to sort out why an 82 year old man with cancer leaves his assisted living home in sunny Arizona, goes to a hotel, shoots a woman in cold blood, and then gets a cab. Something was seriously off about this one, much more so than the two other incidents involving Russians that had been reported to her the previous day. She intended to catch this guy and ask him about it herself.

Even though special interest in this case came from higher up the federal power structure than was typical for Lopez, she had not been provided any real information from the other departments to go on other than that there could be a Russian "connection" to the attacks. Not a lot of help, so far.

Sitting in an otherwise vacant floor of offices in the early morning staring at her computer, she pulled up the information Detective Lineman had sent over and looked at it again. She scrolled down to the make, model, and tag number of the rental car the Russian had leased. Before she had left the previous night, the FBI's high tech video surveillance lab had zeroed in on the rental car and found it on a few traffic cameras around Phoenix. Lopez couldn't help but chuckle every time one of those reports came in, thinking of Lineman's complaints about sifting through hours of video himself. Pieced together, the videos ultimately showed the Russian's rental car heading onto north bound Interstate 17.

Lopez checked her e-mail. More footage with notes was waiting in her in-box. It showed the car had exited onto east bound Interstate 40 at Flagstaff. The Russian had a good head-start, but Lopez figured the techs working at this pace on the video footage from the Interstate cameras ought to have an idea of where he was, or at least where he exited I-40, very soon. Maybe even before breakfast.

"And now he's heading my way," she thought, itching for the opportunity to locate this man and apprehend him.

Chapter 44

EOD Mobile Unit
Arlington, Virginia
5:10 a.m.

Master Chief McAbee stepped into the brightly lit EOD trailer to see petty officers busy at computers and closed the door behind him. The video monitors on the wall were set to various news feeds, all of which displayed the video of the V-1 that the college kids had taken with energetic commentary raging along with it.

"And I thought the sea of reporters was bad when we began this job," McAbee said aloud to no one in particular, "but that mob out there now? They're like a bunch of starved piranhas!"

McAbee took a moment to take in the various news feeds and ascertained that the reporters were jazzed up, and certainly were aiming to get their viewers whipped up into a frenzy. That energy showed in the street outside, as well. Already at that early hour it was clear to see the speculation and political finger pointing spinning the story over the airwaves this way and that. Soon, when the sun broke in the east and the nation began to fully awaken, this bit of news would consume the minds of Americans. The news networks would see to it that they wouldn't get a break from it, either, he thought. He noticed Lieutenant Schmitt leaning against a counter staring off into space looking like he wasn't feeling very well.

"Lieutenant," McAbee said, approaching the Officer in Charge.

"Well, Master Chief," Schmitt replied, "this thing is spiraling out of control. That footage of the missile has gone viral and the pressure is on to figure out what to do next."

"With all due respect," McAbee said, "we provided accurate information about the nature of this missile amazingly early-on considering the circumstances. Clearly we were correct. What they did with it—or didn't do with it—isn't on us. So where do we stand with regard to the current situation? It seems like our work here should be winding down."

Knock, knock, knock.

McAbee shot Schmitt a quizzical expression. Schmitt returned a pale, dreadful look.

"Knocking...that's a first," McAbee said. "I'll get it."

The Master Chief walked to the other end of the trailer and opened the door. Standing outside was a slender woman with shoulder length brunette hair who wore the quintessential blue nylon jacket with "FBI" in yellow letters on the front and sleeves. He could see she packed a sidearm just visible under the open jacket. She looked at McAbee with probing brown eyes that gave him the feeling she could sum him up in about five seconds, and be right about it.

"This EOD?" she asked.

"Yes mam," McAbee replied. "I'm Master Chief Rick McAbee. Please come in."

"Tell you what," the agent said, glancing past him into the trailer, "maybe you'd just step outside? I just have a couple of quick questions."

McAbee had no idea where this was going, but had no reason to deny her request.

"Sure," he said, stepping down out of the trailer and closing the door behind him.

"I'm agent Cecelia Lopez with the FBI," she said brandishing her I.D. as they stepped a little further from the trailer. "And here's the thing...I work right over there [Lopez pointed across the blast zone and the Potomac River to Washington D.C. visible in the distance], and I can't get answers. I'm trying to do my job, I'm being told to get certain things done from higher up, but then no one can answer even some basic questions to help in my investigation. When I look out of my office window, I see this blast zone. So I decided to just drive over here and ask you fellas a few questions myself to see if I can get some answers."

"Agent Lopez, I appreciate your predicament," McAbee said. "Perhaps you should speak with my Lieutenant? He's just inside. I'll...."

"No," Lopez cut him off. "I'm done with getting passed around, and I especially do not want to talk to anyone up the food chain; that's getting me nowhere. Master Chief, obviously I've seen the footage this morning of the missile that made this mess, and I'm guessing they're right about it being a German V-1 type of missile."

"I can't comment on that, I'm afraid," McAbee replied.

"And I'm going to level with you here, between us," she fired at him, her eyes now like laser beams directed at his eyes, "I am after a suspect because the higher-ups have us looking for any Russians who have shown up on the radar with criminal activity in the past two days. Now Master Chief McAbee, you're a capable EOD guy or you wouldn't be here at this site doing this job. So tell me, that V-1, that wouldn't happen to be a Russian weapon that was launched against us, would it?"

The Master Chief averted his gaze from her piercing stare and shifted his weight from one leg to the other.

"Before you answer," Lopez continued, "let me inquire further...I don't suppose it could have been launched by old—and when I say old, I mean in their 80s old—sleeper agents, could it?"

McAbee looked back into her eyes, his own eyes brightening up. His early theory on the nature of this attack had been substantiated by finding the launch site in West Virginia with the old deceased fellow, but having this young FBI agent arriving at the same conclusion by working a different angle was somewhat gratifying.

There was a lengthy pause. McAbee knew he should tow the official line. Lopez knew she should be hearing the official line.

"Agent Lopez," McAbee said slowly and deliberately, "may I ask you a question?"

"Yes."

"Do you think you have a suspect who is going to commit an attack on the United States?"

The Master Chief's question turned the conversation on its head. Now it was Lopez who knew she shouldn't discuss an active investigation outside of her sphere of cleared personnel—but, that was exactly what she was asking McAbee to do.

The pause between them lingered. They stood there looking at each other, sizing each other up, and considering the professional implications of what to do. Finally, Lopez's posture visible softened.

"Yes," she said.

"Then between you, me, and the fence post...yes, you're right on target with your thinking," McAbee offered. "I really can't discuss it, as you know, but I want you to do whatever you can to get ahead of any more of these guys."

"Well, that's not a lot to go on, McAbee," Lopez said, her mouth curling into a slight smile. "But just to get that much of an answer and know I'm on the right line of thinking is helpful and worth fighting the traffic to get over here."

"It's not much," McAbee agreed, relaxing a bit.

"I'll let you get back to work, then," Lopez said and simply turned on her heel to walk away.

"Lopez?" McAbee said, noticing the big "FBI" across the back of her jacket.

"Yes," she stopped and turned back to face him.

"If you ever take a vacation—get a day off," McAbee said, "I hear Hardy, West Virginia is really nice. They have some awesome remote hiking spots in the mountains out that way. Very, very remote. You might want to check it out. And, I know for a fact that some FBI agents go there, and have been there recently enjoying the views...so you ought to be able to find out plenty about vacationing in the area."

Lopez's brow wrinkled into a frown at first as she shot him a look that said she wondered where that randomness came from. Then her expression relaxed, her eyes twinkled, and her cheeks puffed up a little as her mouth bent upwards into a smile.

"I'll do that, Master Chief...I'll do that for sure. Thanks!"

Chapter 45

JFK Airport
New York
10:55 a.m.

Gene called Jeb the moment the plane landed. Talking on his personal cell phone on a crowded plane was not the most secure means to provide information about a potential attack on the U.S. to the CIA, but there was no time to delay. Unfortunately, Jeb did not answer.

"Jeb, I need to speak with you NOW!" Gene said on his voice mail. "I just landed in New York and we have an extremely urgent situation. CALL ME!"

Gene thought for a few moments as he stood and pushed his way into the flow of passengers in the aisle attempting to de-plane. He knew domestic situations needed to be routed to the FBI or Homeland Security, but he did not know who to contact over there and this was gravely serious. Making a mess of things wouldn't help, and there simply was no time to delay. Somebody had to get to Flushing Airfield now.

Gene tried Jeb again.

"CALL ME!" he said again into Jeb's voice mail.

Gene's mind raced, even as his body was trapped in the crushing jam of bodies in the plane's center aisle, trying to think about what to do next.

If he rented a car and drove to Flushing Airfield he'd not have time to get there before noon Eastern Time. If he couldn't get Jeb, he could call the other authorities, but they would never get there in time either. Then it struck him...he was at JFK. What he needed right now was a plane. He could fly to Flushing Airfield and make it there in time to see about stopping this potential nuclear catastrophe if he could find a plane and "borrow" it. If he was wrong, he would probably lose his pilot's license and who knows what other legal troubles would plague him...but the chance he was right was much too great.

Gene finally made it to the doorway, out of the plane, and onto the jet bridge. A door was open in the space just outside of the plane. A few carry on bags were sitting there on the floor. Gene figured the last few passengers had to leave their carry ons there for loading in the storage in the belly of the plane and that they were being provided for pick up at the same spot now as they left the plane.

Gene stepped over the small bags and slipped out through the door. In the madness of passengers trying to hurry out of the plane and make connecting flights, he managed his exit from the jet bridge without anyone paying much attention to him. Once outside, it was a lovely fall morning. The sunlight and chilly air had a somewhat calming affect on Gene as he swiftly and deliberately walked down a set of metal stairs and headed away from the plane along the outside of the terminal. The timing had been lucky and he didn't bump into anyone as he walked away from the plane and tried to get his bearings. He needed to get to some part of the airport where there were smaller aircraft.

Chapter 46

Washington, D.C.
10:55 a.m.

"Mac," Agent Lopez said in a voice that did nothing to hide her agitation, "what's this deal going on in Hardy, West Virginia?"

"Uh..." was the reply she got from her boss, letting her know she had scored a bulls eye.

"Is that all you've got for me?" she shot at him. "Honestly, you've got me working to find potential Russian sleeper agents because the country is under attack, and you don't even provide me with the full information we have on this unfolding situation—information the FBI has because we are the ones investigating it? What's up with that?"

"Now Cecelia," Mac Rogers shot back at her, "there are certain unusual protocols that have been put in place due to the nature of national security on this...."

"Don't give me that!" she vented. "So what do we know, Mac?"

"Okay...just come by my office and we'll talk. But don't get too excited; I probably know less than you think, and what I do know probably will help you less than you hope."

"You know that any little bit of information can make all the difference, Mac. I'll be there within an hour."

"I doubt it."

"What? Why's that?"

"They've been trying to track your Russian and discovered his car on video on I-78 heading towards New York City some time ago," Mac said. "The techs keep finding him with such a delay that when local law enforcement get the message he's already down the road somewhere else. They are sending you an update to your phone now. I'm guessing you want to head north and see about him?"

"You're darn right I do," Lopez shot back at him. "If he's that close I'm taking a helicopter right now and heading up there myself. But I will come by to see you when I get back."

"I don't doubt that, Agent Lopez...."

Chapter 47

JFK Airport
New York
11:15 a.m.

JFK airport was massive and busy. The situation worked for Gene, helping him remain undetected as he roamed around outside the terminals. It worked against him in that he had to find somewhere with smaller aircraft if he hoped to commandeer a plane to fly to Flushing Airfield, and he had no idea where to go to accomplish this.

Gene just kept walking around jumbo jets, regional jets, vehicles pulling baggage cars, fuel trucks, and every kind of airport busy-ness imaginable like he knew where he was going. He hoped that carrying an air of authority in his step would help avoid suspicion if someone did notice him walking around.

As he got to the outskirts of one side of the airport near some of the jet maintenance facilities, he noticed some parked Cessnas and Beechcrafts. A few mechanics were at work around the smaller planes. Then, as he rounded the corner of a hanger to get a better look around, he saw it. There parked among the smaller aircraft sat a P-51 Mustang D-30. Its silvery metal body shone brightly in the morning sun. A mechanic was collecting some tools off of the ground, a gesture that made Gene think he had just finished up working on the motor.

The mechanic then spun on his heel and walked around the wing.

Gene got as close as he could, hanging around the tail of a Cessna pretending to inspect the elevators as he watched the activity around the P-51 closely.

Gene could not believe his luck; the mechanic stepped onto the wing of the old warbird, climbed in the cockpit, and started the engine. The propeller spun slowly, the engine coughed a couple of times, and then roared to life.

The mechanic set the throttle to an idle and then climbed back out of the airplane.

Gene's whole body tightened. He watched the scene like a hawk on the branch of a tree watches a mouse scurrying below.

Then it happened...the mechanic picked up a handful of tools from the ground near the plane and walked away towards the hanger.

Gene's mind and body went on autopilot. He was both elated to have this chance to get to Flushing airfield in time and in style—if he could get away with "borrowing" the plane—and deeply disturbed at what he was about to do.

In a single motion that was quite deft for an old, retired agent, Gene dropped his carry-on bag, sprinted to the idling P-51, grabbed the wheel chocks from both wheels underneath the wings, hopped up on the left wing, climbed into the cockpit, and sat down. He eyed the fuel gauge...full. He clipped himself in, throttled up, and taxied off.

"Drive it like you stole it, Gene!" he advised himself aloud. "Because you did, you crazy geezer!"

Chapter 48

FBI Helicopter
11:38 a.m.

Agent Lopez wasted no time. The many resources at her disposal for pursuing the Russian fugitive included an FBI helicopter, and soon she was in the air headed northeast straight for New York City.

On route, she was running the operation to apprehend the Russian from her cell phone with the New York field office. There had been some delays in finding the fugitive's car on the Interstate surveillance video feeds.

"Why are we still finding this guy on old footage and not right on him now?" Lopez asked the New York agent who was tasked with heading-up the video search.

"It's been a needle in a haystack, Agent Lopez," he shot back at her. "We're lucky we found him at all last night and have a good idea of his recent movements."

"Well, what can you tell me?" she asked.

"Less than 15 minutes ago we have him getting off of 278 in Astoria right by LaGuardia."

"What?" Lopez exclaimed. "Get the local cops on this guy... top priority!"

"Already done," the agent replied. "Nothing to report as yet, though."

"We're heading towards LaGuardia," Lopez said, "and will be right over the area in a few minutes."

Chapter 49

Flushing Airport
New York City
11:55 a.m.

Vassily had driven most of the night. A thrill had shot through him when New York City had come into view up ahead in the morning light as he had approached it from the west.

"I never thought I would see this sight again," Vassily thought as he drove along.

The heavy morning traffic had made him feel safer and better hidden but also anxious and trapped. Once he was over a bridge and in Astoria, he had gotten off the Interstate and made his way along many smaller roads to College Point.

Finally, he saw what had been Flushing Airport. The overgrown, sizable chunk of land was obvious, and in the late morning there was no traffic around the area. The old Russian easily found a gated entrance chained and locked on the road Lindon Place that led into the property.

Vassily pulled the rental car up to the chain-link gate. He got out and used a pair of bolt cutters he had thought to purchase at a hardware store back in Arkansas to cut open the chain that locked the gate. He quickly drove the car through the gate, took the time to close it behind him, and then drove down the long forsaken section of Linden Place. Vassily had worried that someone would see him breaking into the property, but no one had been around or driven past. Vassily chuckled gleefully as the car soon was out of sight from the surrounding areas as the marshy land around the road provided an excellent cover of tall weeds and brush.

The road quickly deteriorated into a marshy mess with water covering the old pavement in many spots. Vassily worried that the car would get stuck, but it made its way through to the old tarmac runway. As he drove out of the weeds and onto the north end of the runway there suddenly came into view what Vassily had dreamed of many times over the years...the Yak-9 he would fly for his mission.

Vassily noticed the black three-blade propeller, the light gray colored underbelly, and the two-tone green camouflage pattern paint job on the top side of the old war bird with the bright red Soviet star on the fuselage behind the wing. A pride swelled within him as he admired the sight. The tires were muddy from the plane's recent landing at the old airfield.

But his emotional moment was cut short by a man, easily Vassily's age, who quickly approached his car.

"Comrade," Vassily said.

"Comrade," the other man replied.

Vassily pushed the button that popped open the trunk. Together they lifted the RA115 and carried it to the Yak fighter. The aircraft was fitted with some cables underneath the fuselage and the suitcase sized device was outfitted with small rings that attached the device neatly to the plane.

There was urgency in both men's actions but the other man took time to double check the connections.

"Good luck, comrade," the man said to Vassily in Russian.

"To you, too," he replied in their native tongue. "The keys are in the car and there is a weapon in the passenger's seat and grenades in the bag in case you should need them."

"By the way, that ShVAK 20 mm cannon," the fellow said, grinning widely, "it's real. And so are the 120 rounds for it. The 12.7 mm machine gun is original equipment as well, comrade. 170 rounds are ready for it. I thought they might come in handy!"

Vassily smiled back at him, then climbed across a wing and into the cockpit and fired up the Yak-9.

Chapter 50

Flushing Airport
New York City
12:07 p.m.

The local police working with the FBI had all available units in Brooklyn and Queens searching for the car Vassily had been driving, and checkpoints had been set up around those areas. A police helicopter helped in the search, circling the area overhead.

Vassily's accomplice knew he did not want to go far in the rental car in case the authorities had any reason to be searching for his comrade. He had another car parked just a few blocks away from the abandoned airfield.

The man got into the rental car and smiled when he saw the stubby little version of an AK-47 in the passenger's seat along with an entire duffle bag packed with full clips and grenades. They would make a nice addition to his collection, he thought.

He started the car and took off across the runway, glimpsing out of the driver's side window at the Yak with its spinning propeller as he headed for the road that Vassily had used to access the runway. Once on the road, the tall weeds blocked his view of the plane.

"Ah, good luck on your mission, Comrade!" he thought.

At the perimeter fence, he stopped the car, quickly got out, and swung the gate open. Before he could get back to the car, a police car came driving along the road. It's lights began flashing and the siren whooped a quick burst.

The man made a dash for the passenger's door, grabbed the stubby AK-47 and bag, and ran, disappearing into the tall weeds.

"Stop. Put your hands in the air and STOP!" an officer's voice boomed out over a loud speaker from the police car.

The police cruiser pulled inside the open gate and stopped just long enough for an officer to hop out of the passenger's side, pull his pistol, and dash after the man on foot into the tall weeds. The police car took off, swerved around the rental car, and sped down the abandoned stretch of road, the driver hoping to find a way to get around to the other side of the weeds and cut of the fugitive's flight.

"This is unit 36...we have a car matching the description of the wanted vehicle at a gate to an abandoned property at 23rd Avenue and Lindon Place," the officer called over the radio. "The driver has fled on foot into the property and appears to be armed."

The police dispatcher echoed the report over the radio with a call for all available units to go to the abandoned property for backup. Sirens wailed and lights flashed all over College Point as units raced to the scene.

The police helicopter was over the scene immediately. Agent Lopez and the crew of the FBI helicopter had been patched into the local police dispatch radio and heard the news. They were a few minutes away and approaching the scene.

"He disappeared into the tall weeds on foot," Lopez heard over the headset she now wore. "He is heading to the interior of the property. Officer is pursuing on...I hear shots! Shots fired! Repeat, shots fired! Holy smokes. There's a plane taking off in here. It's like some kind of...of...old fighter plane."

Lopez clearly heard an automatic weapon firing a short burst in the background as the officer was transmitting his report over the radio.

"All units be advised, we have shots fired at the scene and an airplane is reported moving on the property," the dispatcher broadcast.

"This is Air Unit Four, I have eyes on the plane. It's taking off, heading down the runway in a northerly direction. We are sticking with the ground units to look for this guy...woh, we're taking fire! Suspect is well armed! A small explosion...there's a small...he must have grenades!"

"Units be advised, the suspect is heavily armed and dangerous, including what appears to be grenades. Repeat, he is armed with both a gun and grenades."

Lopez was trying to take in the information and sort it quickly. Why would there be an airplane at an abandoned airfield? And for him to be armed with grenades? The Russian murderer coming all this way, top priority given to her to hunt him down, the recent attacks on Washington, D.C.—now a small plane at an abandoned runway in New York City.... It was adding up to something really bad and something really big.

"Stick with the plane," Lopez said to the FBI helicopter pilot beside her. "Stick with the plane."

Chapter 51

Flushing Airport
New York City
12:12 p.m.

Gene had climbed the P-51-D-30 at a steep angle when taking off from JFK and flying north towards Flushing Airfield near College Point, New York. The deserted airfield was just east across Flushing Bay from busy LaGuardia Airport. Tons of air traffic would be criss-crossing the area, but Gene wasn't sure if the busy airspace would help or hinder his efforts to find the sleeper agent's plane and avoid being intercepted himself.

Gene had turned off the transponder in the P-51 back at JFK to avoid being easily traced by air traffic control. Now he reached over and turned off his radio too, figuring he might as well concentrate on the task at hand rather than be side-tracked by the air traffic controllers who already were trying in vain to contact him. He couldn't help but think about how to explain his way out of stealing a P-51 for a joy ride if he was wrong about the attack and the sleeper agent. He would know shortly if he was soon going to be a big problem for the authorities, or if his intel was going to pay off and he'd be able to justify his actions.

Gene had considered flying low to attempt to avoid radar, but his fighter pilot instincts kicked in and he went for altitude superiority over his potential foe. He also instinctively flew into position to approach Flushing Field with the sun in the southern sky to his back.

At 10,000 feet and approaching the area of Flushing Field, he could see LaGuardia Airport about a mile off to his left. Gene scanned the ground below him, and there it was, a large triangular thicket of green land without housing, large enough that it easily stood out among the congestion of the surrounding neighborhoods. The airstrip, likewise, was easily spotted. Although from the air, after years with no maintenance, the paved runway no longer looked like a straight strip. The untidy visual effect from its neglect was made all the more obvious by the crisply edged two-lane highway running parallel to the runway just outside the airport. The old runway looked more like a mosaic of dirt and tarmac with a little vegetation thrown in for good measure and a big puddle in the middle. This place was a strangely deserted island of aviation history, right under the nose of LaGuardia, smack in the middle of a residential area.

Gene glanced at his watch...12:22. Was he too late? Maybe the time in the message wasn't Eastern Time? Or maybe he had it all wrong? But his gut was telling him he was right. He decided to take a closer look at the airfield, coming out of the sun in a slight dive. Gaining speed, he scanned the airfield and all around the skies close to it.

"What are you going to do if he is there, Gene?" he asked himself aloud. "Strafe the guy?"

He had no weapons on the old warbird. Luckily, he assumed, his foe wouldn't either—how could he? He could drop that suitcase nuke from any Cessna or Beachcraft, or any old plane, so in the P-51 Gene might certainly overwhelm him with speed and performance, but so what?

And even if he did have real .50 cals on his plane, being a retired CIA agent would hardly give him permission to attack someone in New York hanging out on an abandoned air strip on a hunch.

But the attacks on D.C. were proof that this intel could be about a real threat, and it all added up. Not to do something would be impossible for Gene to live with if this turned out to be another attack, especially a nuclear bomb in downtown New York. And finding out about this threat so late in the game simply left him no time to work things through channels. He'd just have to figure it out as he went along.

"Flying by the seat of your pants again, eh?" Gene muttered and chuckled.

He continued to pick up speed in his dive and looked hard ahead at the old runway as he raced towards it. Nothing stood out at first. Then, it caught his eye. A plane, low and climbing, had just taken off from Flushing Field and was heading northwest to go out over the East River. If he had been a minute later, Gene thought, he would not have been able to know for sure that plane was the one he was looking for. The realization gave him great relief for choosing to "borrow" the P-51, and not wait a second later.

If the decoded message was right, the guy was heading for Wall Street. Even as Gene was assessing the situation, the plane was gaining speed and altitude fast as it flew over Rikers Island, staying just north of LaGuardia. Then it headed southwest towards Manhattan.

Gene, perhaps by instinct, or just for lack of a better idea, banked left and followed through on the dive just as if he were going to open up on the beam of the bogey with his guns and shoot him down.

"What in the world?" Gene said aloud in astonishment when he got closer to the other airplane. "That's a Yak-9!"

Gene's mind raced. First, the information that Washington, D.C. had come under attack from a Soviet version of a V-1 rocket. Now, New York was experiencing an attack carried out by a World War II era Soviet fighter. It was just too bizarre! Even factoring in the likelihood of long-deployed sleeper agents carrying out these attacks, the time warp was surreal. The realities of a by-gone era seemed to be clashing with the modern world. And the twist in this plot, Gene thought, was that the only one who knew about this most horrific attack so far was flying around in an unarmed P-51-D-30 in hot pursuit. It all just added up to the weirdest thing ever. What he wouldn't give for those .50 cal machines guns right now....

But as it turned out, even if those guns still had graced the wings of his plane, Gene would not have had a shot. His adversary saw him dropping in from the sun. Gene wasn't sure how he could have, especially since it was unlikely that pilot could have thought anyone was on to him at this stage of the game.

"This guy is the real deal," Gene thought to himself.

***

Vassily, out of old habit, had swiveled his head on the end of his neck from the second his plane left the ground. Maybe it was the stress of again being on a real mission. Or perhaps, it was just old training kicking in. Either way he was very surprised when his constant scanning of the sky, particularly towards the sun, revealed a fighter bearing down on him.

Old reflexes shot through his body. He ruddered instantly, jammed the stick, and broke hard to the right. He hoped the other plane would overshoot him. He fingered for the trigger on the stick, itching for the chance at a shot if the other plane whipped past him with the speed from its dive.

***

Gene, at the last second, as he was about to mash a trigger

that would probably do nothing anyway, saw the Yak break hard to the right. He banked down to the right, cutting the throttle and throwing on the flaps to keep from overshooting, staying behind the Yak to get his guns on him. The P-51 slowed and he managed to stay behind his foe, following the Yak into a circle now somewhere over New York City.

Both planes were banked in a hard clockwise turn. The G-forces tugged at Gene's body causing him to groan as he turned for all he was worth, trying to pull inside of his foe for a shot.

***

"Viper Control, this is Bulldog One," the F-16 pilot said over the radio. "We have a visual. You're not going to believe this, but that Bogey—it's a P-51. Repeat, a P-51. It is engaging another plane. What the....he's engaging what looks like a Soviet Yak fighter right over Midtown Manhattan! It's a dogfight, fellas. No joke! It's a dogfight and these guys are serious! Is there some kind of air show going on? What the heck is this all about?"

"Negative, Bulldog One," the controller's voice responded. "No show. These yahoos are on their own."

"Bulldog One, this is Viper Control Actual," a new voice, the commander's, came over the jet fighters' headsets. "We're not taking any chances. Permission to arm. Bulldog One on the original bogey. Bulldog Two, you're on the Yak. Prepare to fire, but hold your fire. Repeat, prepare to fire but hold and do not fire. Get in close and let them know you're onto them. See if they break it up and acknowledge."

"Roger that...they're in a turning circle, sir, right over Rockefeller Center. I swear, it's like something straight out of World War Two! Looks like the Yak is starting to turn inside the P-51."

***

With his flaps deployed, Gene began to try to close in behind the Yak-9. He turned with the Yak at first, but after the second full circle made by both planes, each after the other, the P-51 began bleeding off too much speed. Gene closed the flaps and throttled up, knowing that while his plane was an excellent match to his opponent's in many ways, the Yak soon would out turn him in this scenario if the other pilot could handle the Gs.

On the third circle the P-51 lost a little more ground. On the fourth, the Yak turned inside of Gene and then, the unlikely happened. A flurry of 20 millimeter cannon and 12.7 millimeter machine gun rounds crackled and whizzed by his canopy, complete with brilliant white tracers burning in brightly arced streaks just over his head.

Pop! Pieces of canopy flew around Gene just as he heard a metallic thunk and felt the concussion of a round hitting the armor plating behind his head.

"Argh!" Gene shouted at the instantaneous realization that he was in a dogfight with a fully armed Yak.

***

"Holy cow! The Yak is armed! Repeat...the Yak is armed. No joke; he just sent a burst of rounds within inches of the P-51. No wait...the back of the bubble canopy took a hit...Bulldog Two requesting permission to fire on the Yak!"

"Negative," the commander replied. "Break them up and see if you can get a visual on the pilots, but stay armed and alert. We've got a whole city of people directly below all this—can you get along side of them and wake them up."

"Negative, sir. It's a prop plane turn fight. Can't get in there with this bird."

***

Gene instinctively inverted his plane and pulled back on the stick, to perform a spilt-S maneuver, diving for the deck and reversing his direction while pulling underneath his adversary. A quick glance at the gauges showed everything was fine. Hopefully, the back glass was the only hit, Gene thought, and lucky that it must have been a machine gun round and not one of those beefy 20 mil cannon rounds!

The city's straight streets and rectangular buildings seemed to come right up at him. He dove nearly onto what he figured must be 6th Avenue, and could easily see the red, green, and yellow of traffic lights on the side streets as his plane's Merlin engine roared along right over top of the street below him. Then, he pulled the plane up and hard to the right and he pushed the throttle wide open triggering the War Emergency Power.

For some reason the insane scenario he found himself in made Gene's mind wander even as he jockeyed the plane for his life and tried to think of a way to turn the fight to his favor and get a reversal on the Yak. He thought of William Overstreet, Jr., a Virginia boy from Clifton Forge who was the World War II pilot who chased a German BF 109 quite amazingly right under the Eiffel Tower's arches in his P-51 Mustang during a dogfight in 1944—another one of those bits of history etched in his mind.

***

Vassily was aggravated that he had missed the P-51. He didn't have any more time to be distracted from his mission. He was thinking that there was no way the P-51 could have guns. It must be a warbird from an air show—but how did it show up here? And why would the pilot attack him? To just appear like that over Flushing Airfield at that moment, it was as if his nemesis knew where to find him. But that was impossible. If the P-51 pilot knew about his mission, why hadn't he called it in the authorities? They surely wouldn't come to get him in a Mustang. It was insane.

But, Vassily was a fighter pilot at heart, and he couldn't stave off his desire to finish this guy. He was only a few minutes away from his target. Plus, he could release his package at any time and it would be a successful mission, although Vassily was not one to miss his mark—oh no, he would get to Wall Street and vaporize the stock exchange just as he had dreamed of for so many years. Even so, he reckoned he would make time to finish one last dogfight.

As Vassily dove after the P-51, he had to watch his speed. He knew that high speeds and G-forces would rip the Yak's wings right off the plane if he wasn't careful, so he had to throttle back. That allowed the Mustang to gain some distance on him as he watched it nearly plummet into a busy street.

Vassily followed and felt for his trigger as the Mustang was right on the verge of entering his sights again.

***

Gene was still thinking about Overstreet and the extraordinary Eiffel Tower moment when his mind and body reflexively finished the maneuver. He fire-walled the throttle, sweeping the P-51 into a barrel roll that took him up, over, and around the Yak. It clearly surprised his foe and had the desired reversal; the Soviet plane on its straight trajectory blasted past Gene, overshooting him. In an instant, Gene leveled out the Mustang right behind the Yak, put the gun sight pipper dead on him, and squeezed the trigger.

To his surprise, the guns barked to life, audible even over the roar of the Merlin engine. In the periphery of both eyes he saw flames emit from the front edges of both wings. For a second, he waited expectantly for the Yak to burst into bits. The Yak was dead-center in the sighting pipper and there was no was no way that a burst mass from six .50 cals was going to miss that shot.

The Yak broke off to the left, dove, and began running along, ducking and weaving, at rooftop level over the city buildings with Gene in full-on pursuit. It was then that Gene came to the realization that he had done no damage to the Yak because the Mustang was outfitted with a clever arrangement used in air shows these days. His machine guns were equipped with propane gas fired guns that made very realistic sounding shots, and even gave off an authentic flash when they fired. But no bullets....

***

"What a pilot!" Bulldog One said over the radio. "Man, that P-51 pilot just pulled an amazing reversal and got guns on the Yak. I saw him fire, but the Yak took no damage...his guns have to be fakes because he had the Yak dead-to-rights. Whew...okay, Yak is on the run south ducking and weaving over Greenwich Village with the P-51 in pursuit. Maybe it's just me, but I can't help wanting to take out the Yak and assist the American plane. Bulldog Two, now that they're running more straight let's break up this fight."

"Roger, Bulldog One. Bulldog Two going in to come alongside the Yak."

"Roger, I'll come alongside the P-51 and see what this guy looks like."

The powerful fighter jets blasted forward and took the opportunity to fly close beside their respective bogeys. The momentousness of two piston engine fighters from the top of the food chain of their era, and two modern jet fighters, flying at roof-top level along downtown Manhattan created pandemonium below. Buildings and cars shook as the concussion from the engines created earthquake-intense seismic rumbles through the city just feet beneath them. Thousands of onlookers were shocked. Traffic snarled into knots. The news agencies didn't need to be called—they had heard the ruckus themselves and were immediately attempting to get some kind of video footage of this attack, or whatever it was, and go live on the air with it before it was over.

Bulldog One blasted in close beside the P-51.

"P-51, you have been intercepted," the F-16 pilot broadcast over a spectrum of aviation frequencies.

Bulldog One was then able to see the nose art on the old American warbird—a pinup girl stretched out and the words, "Hard to Get," above her. The F-16 pilot laughed.

"Repeat," he said, pointing to the side of his helmet where his right ear was located to indicate for the P-51 pilot to listen in on the radio, "P-51, 'Hard to Get,' you certainly are that! If you can hear me, acknowledge and rock your wings."

Bulldog One knew the air traffic controllers had been attempting to contact the P-51 pilot ever since they picked him up leaving JFK. But, as odd as the situation was, he followed the same protocol he would for any rogue plane in a restricted airspace and hoped that the capable fighter pilot in the other plane would have a working radio and help end this episode before they had to end it for him.

***

The F-16 roaring up beside Gene caught him by surprise. He had been so fixated on the Yak that he hadn't seen the jet approaching him from behind. Just then, another F-16 blew past him in pursuit of the Yak, causing the P-51 to shudder in its wake. The fighter jet to Gene's left was matching his speed and they were canopy to canopy. Gene could see the jet pilot's black bubble face shield and gray helmet, and he figured it was time to turn his radio back on.

Gene held up his left hand, keeping his right one on the stick, and then reached down with it, turned on his radio, and held his hand up again as if to surrender.

"F-16, this is the P-51, do you read me," Gene said.

"P-51, this is the F-16 to your left—rock your wings and acknowledge."

Gene did.

"The Yak has a nuclear device—he's going after Wall Street. I'm retired CIA agent Gene Davis. I'll stand down, but you've got to get that Yak!"

"Gene Davis! What the..." a familiar voice came over the radio.

"Frank?" Gene said over the radio. "Frank McDonald. Well, fancy meeting you here!"

"This is Viper Control Actual...Gene, get out of there. Follow Bulldog One; he will escort you. Why am I not surprised that if there was a Yak dogfighting a P-51 over Manhattan, one of the pilots would be you? Bulldog One, escort 'Agent Davis' back to base."

"This is P-51, roger. Following the Fighting Falcon."

"Bulldog One here, roger...follow on my right, P-51."

The F-16 with its smaller, older sibling tagging along in formation on its right—shattered back canopy, pin-up girl nose art, and all—banked left and headed towards the river.

***

Vassily was aggravated. He knew the P-51 pilot had out flown him. If those guns had been real, that pilot would have shot him down, no doubt.

"Enough of that," he thought. "I've got to concentrate on my mission."

At that moment he was rocked by the rumble of a fighter jet blasting up alongside of him. Vassily knew he'd need some altitude to escape the nuclear blast when it went off, but then again...he didn't have much time in this world anyway. But he wanted to see the aftermath, to know he'd delivered a major blow to capitalism, and see what his comrades had in store for the future of the revolution! How could he miss such a triumph?

He wanted to know how it would turn out. His mission was likely the one on which the whole plan hinged. It would be the essential move to break the capitalists and hurt them where they were most vulnerable—at their monetary center. He would succeed!

***

"By the way, Bulldog One," Gene said as they banked away from the Yak and the other F-16, "that Yak-9...he's armed. No joke. Your wing mate better watch that one; that pilot knows what he's doing."

"We saw that, Manhattan Mustang." Bulldog One had just coined a new nick name for Gene—as fighter pilots often do. This one had all likelihood of sticking and commemorating this over-the-top dogfight right over top of Rockefeller Center.

"The Yak is breaking right!" a man's voice came over the headset. "I'm attempting to follow—he's rogue! Repeat, he's not acknowledging my intercept and breaking right."

Gene still could see the Yak and the other F-16 off to his right. He watched as the Yak pulled a tight circle and easily came around on the F-16. Bulldog Two nosed straight up just before the Yak got a shot on him trying to use the jet's massive engines to their best advantage against the antique airplane by leaving it in the dust below him. But the Yak followed, climbing very strongly at first.

"He's on me. He's on me!" Bulldog Two's voice came through the headset.

"I'm coming around your way for a shot," Bulldog One said, blasting forward away from the P-51, which rocked violently as the F-16 tore out in front of him towards the Yak. "Mustang, you stay put."

"Yeah, right! In what universe?" Gene said, banking right and firewalling his throttle again back towards the Yak, too.

Gene saw tracers from the Yak 9 streak a vertical white line upwards as the F-16's afterburners kicked in to attempt to rocket up and away from the Yak. The jet jumped ahead but Gene clearly saw the flashes as some of the 20 mil rounds found their mark. The jet belched smoke as it continued its ascent.

"I'm hit! I'm hit."

"This is Viper Control—permission to fire...repeat, Bulldogs you have permission to fire. If you can get guns on him, that'll be better than hitting him with a missile over the city. See if you can wing him. We'd like to interrogate this joker if possible."

"Bulldog One—roger that. Engaging the Yak."

The damaged jet was able to jump well out of gun range of the Yak even with a plume of thick smoke trailing him. The Yak gave up chase and dove back down. About the time the Yak 9 regained the speed he had lost in the climb Bulldog One was on him, lining him up for a shot with his 20 mm Gatling gun.

Gene watched as the Yak deftly denied the jet the chance to get guns on him. This time the Yak performed an Immelman, the pilot pulling back on the stick to take the plane straight up in a tight curve inverted. The Yak, upside-down, flew past the F-16 canopy to canopy before flipping over right-side-up again, heading back in the opposite direction. Bulldog One overshot by a mile and began a right hand turn to try and come around again as the Yak dove back to the rooftops and headed towards the Empire State Building that towered over Midtown Manhattan clearly visible straight ahead of Gene.

Gene flew the Mustang on a path to converge with the Yak just west of the Empire State Building. He could see he would have an excellent deflection shot, if only he had guns. The Yak was now headed south. Gene knew he would be over Union Square in a minute, and then Wall Street was just a mile or two beyond that.

Gene had it straight in his head that Bulldog One was coming around in the northern sky, but he could not see him at this point. There was no time left for this engagement. The edge of the Manhattan peninsula was right in front of them. Gene could see the Brooklyn Bridge ahead in the distance. The Yak lined up following Broadway at full throttle straight southwesterly.

"I'm coming around," Gene heard Bulldog One say. "I can't get a lock on him. I can't get a lock—but I'll have guns in three, two...what! Where'd that helicopter come from...I had to evade a helicopter, a news chopper...you've got to be kidding me! Can I shoot him down? Of all the stupid...."

City Hall was right below Gene who continued to fly on a trajectory to cross paths with the Yak, only a matter of blocks from the Wall Street Stock Exchange. Gene could see the F-16 off to his right trying to come around quickly, and he thought how oddly cumbersome the jet seemed compared to their more nimble prop fighters. Without hesitation, throttle wide open, Gene came in on the Yak, slightly above, behind, and on the Yak's left at a good angle for a deflection shot.

Gene never even thought about it—he just acted. He tilted the P-51 45 degrees counterclockwise as it intersected at an angle with the straight flying Yak 9. The left wing on the Mustang clipped the rudder and right elevator of the Yak, cutting them clean off the tail section as it sped past.

Gene felt the impact, and the P-51 cart wheeled violently. He struggled and was able to right the now listing plane just in time to avoid kissing the top of a building. He looked left out of the shattered cockpit and saw the tip of his left wing crumpled with several metal pieces fluttering in the wind.

"How do those nukes work?" Gene wondered. "If it's armed, would a crashing plane cause detonation?"

Gene thought it might be a little late to consider that question now, but he figured whatever the outcome, trying to stop the attack had to be better than letting the sleeper go through his proper protocol to arm and detonate the bomb.

At this point, Gene was so close to the bomb that he knew he'd never know if it did go off. He nursed the controls and was able to convince the Mustang to bank left and he looked back over his shoulder at the Yak to see what was going on.

His adversary was in a wicked flat spin, careening downwards in a westerly direction. Spinning, spinning...Gene was dizzy just watching and could only imagine the disorienting experience of the pilot in that cockpit. He watched as the plane hit the ground at an angle, skidding across a grassy field. He soon realized the field was by the 9/11 memorial where the Twin Towers had been just 600 feet from the Stock Exchange.

Chapter 52

Manhattan
New York
12:35 p.m.

Agent Lopez shook her head in disbelief. She and the pilot in the FBI helicopter had been stunned to come across two old fighter planes at the abandoned airfield, and had been even more amazed when a dogfight ensued. They had been helpless in the helicopter to do anything but fly around and watch the events unfold. It had been like being right there in a World War II air battle, except that Rockefeller Center, the Empire State Building, and the Brooklyn Bridge were the backdrops—and, of course, the pair of modern fighter jets that had suddenly burst onto the scene to try and break up the fight and intercept the old fighters. It had been crazy, all out, military air combat right over Manhattan!

In the midst of the melee, Lopez had kept in mind that her pursuit was for the murder suspect that she had been tracking across the United States. Her hunch had been that her fugitive was piloting the plane with the red star on the side that had taken off from the abandoned airfield rather than the guy in the shoot-out back by the rental car—so she and the helicopter pilot had stuck with the plane.

Lopez and the helicopter pilot had chased the battle the best they could with all that transpired at break-neck speeds. And they had been close enough to the action at the end of the air battle to see the two old fighter planes collide.

Lopez watched in awe as the plane with the damaged wing regained control and flew off. But the plane she was pursuing went into a flat spin and crashed onto the ground between the north and south 9/11 Memorial Pools. She had the pilot put the helicopter down in a clearing between some rows of trees near the 9/11 South Memorial Pool.

Lopez sprang from the helicopter and dashed towards the plane wreckage. The fighter had skidded up against some trees. The right wing was ripped off but the fuselage was intact. She jumped up onto the remaining wing and could see an old man slumped in the seat inside the cockpit, apparently unconscious.

***

Having watched the Yak spin down and crash by the spot where the Twin Towers had stood, Gene winced in expectation. Tic, tic, tic…the seconds went by but to Gene's enormous relief no blast occured.

"How fitting that he should end up at the 9/11 site in a crumpled heap," Gene thought, relaxing more all the time as he became increasingly confident that the nuclear bomb might not detonate.

Gene noticed a black helicopter hovering over the crash site. He circled back around, the P-51 wanting to list to one side with its tattered wingtip, but otherwise easily controlled. Orders were coming across his radio from the jet pilot assigned to escort him back to his base, but he couldn't help himself. The four-lane-wide and very straight road just adjacent to the 9/11 Memorial site was mostly clear. Impulsively, he circled around, cut the throttle, lowered the landing gear, and landed the P-51 right in the middle of the north bound side of West Street.

Gene killed the engine, threw open what was left of the shattered cockpit canopy, and ran to the wreckage of the Yak. As he approached, a young woman with "FBI" in yellow letters on her jacket already was on the scene and working to get the Yak's canopy open. Gene, well acquainted with Yaks, stepped up onto the wing and did it for her.

"Stay back," she told him. "I'm agent Lopez with the FBI and you need to clear this area."

Crack!

The shot was close, sudden, and deafening.

Agent Lopez flew backwards off the wing and crumpled onto the ground. Reflexively, Gene grabbed the old Russian's arm and smacked it hard against the edge of the fuselage. The Makarov pistol dropped from Vassily's hand, hit the wing, and slid to the ground.

"You! You old fool!" Gene exclaimed in Russian.

"Me, ha!" Vassily shot back at him, his head a bit wobbly from the crash but with determination in his eyes. "You can't stop it now. I may have failed, but The Revolution is upon you, American!"

"No," Gene said to the Russian, noticing one leg of the old man's pants soaked in fresh blood. "You deluded fool! You don't know who you are working for, do you?"

"Of course I do," the Russian managed to whisper, his eyes now blinking as he fought to keep them open. "There is only one way we could be activated!"

"No," Gene said deliberately. "Your old comrades sold you out. You old sleepers...your activation info was sold to the highest bidder."

Gene's words seemed to rally Vassily's strength momentarily.

"You lying capitalist!"

"Ha, me lie? What do I have to gain from it? How do you think I knew just where to find you? I just wanted to let you know it was radical Muslim extremists who bought you and your comrades' services. Very likely your Chechen buddies... you're working for them. So, as it turns out, you are indeed just a murdering terrorist."

Gene watched Vassily's eyes as the news sunk in. Even though the old sleeper's mind recoiled from the ghastly thought, the truth of what Gene said to him hit home and he slumped forward against the harness belts as he faded from consciousness.

"Hands in the air, you!" Gene heard a woman's voice from the ground behind him.

"I was just coming to check on you," Gene said, following orders and raising his hands.

Gene turned slowly to see that the agent who had been shot was pointing a pistol at him with one hand, wincing, and holding her free hand on her bulletproof vest just about over her heart.

"I'm sure glad you had that vest on, Agent Lopez!" Gene said, smiling.

"Shut up and get down here," she replied, keeping her aim true.

At that moment, the area flooded with police, fire, and rescue officers pouring in from all directions. Gene slid down off the wing and was handcuffed by a couple of policemen and ushered away to a patrol car as EMTs climbed onto the Yak and began working to help the old Russian sleeper agent. Agent Lopez remained right there by the Yak to oversee the apprehension of her fugitive.

As Gene was stuffed into the back of a police car, he noticed a crowd—many taking videos and photos with their cell phones—had gathered in the street around the parked P-51.

Chapter 53

Lazy G Ranch
Near Salome, Arizona
17 October
11:32 p.m.

Gene drove back onto the ranch in his pick up late at night five days later. Fatigue from recent events, however, did not stop him from standing and gazing up into the massive Arizona sky for some time. The air was perfectly still and the sky clear. The heavens above him were at once deeply dark and moonless and yet brilliant with a billion stars twinkling.

Returning home to so remote a place had a warming, satisfying effect on him.

Fatigue finally won out over star gazing. Gene disrupted the desert's darkness by switching on his flashlight then followed the beam of light into the house and went to bed.

He slept hard, very hard.

The next morning, Gene was up before dawn, too excited to sleep long now that he was back to his much anticipated retirement at the Lazy G Ranch.

He hurriedly dressed, pulled on his boots, zipped up his shotgun chaps over his jeans, grabbed the white rope halter that hung on a peg by the front door, and got his weathered cowboy hat. He put the hat on his head as he walked outside into the chilly desert air.

The twinkling stars, repositioned in the black sky from earlier in the night, greeted Gene again. A faint glow was visible on the horizon to the east, and there was enough light now that he could make out the general landscape around him. The retired agent enjoyed every step he took on the sandy, gravely desert land—the familiar feel of it sort of spongy under his boots.

Dusty greeted Gene by nickering softly and approaching the cowboy as Gene opened a gate and entered the lot. Several other geldings were nearby—some of Gunny's horses at the ranch temporarily—but they were uninterested in the two-legged newcomer and remained standing close to one another about 20 feet away. By the time he had haltered Dusty and was leading the Quarter Horse out through the gate, the sunrise was an orangish glow with a few clouds providing an interesting arrangement of silhouettes. Gene led Dusty down the ranch road that meandered along a wash to the barn.

At the barn, Gene tied Dusty to the hitching rail that ran along one wall just outside the door. Gene shuffled into the tack room and returned with a roping saddle, a saddle pad, a bridle, a lariat, and a brush. He brushed Dusty once over, mainly to make sure there was nothing that might get under the saddle pad and cause trouble. He deftly swung the saddle pad into place and then did the same with the saddle. He grabbed hold of the saddle horn and moved the saddle back and forth a bit to see that it was nestled well onto the horse's back before he cinched it up.

Every little task held great joy for Gene this morning, and the small seemingly mundane business of getting Dusty ready for a ride was pure pleasure for him. When Dusty was all tacked up and Gene was about to mount, the rancher stopped, removed his hat, bowed his head, and prayed.

Gene thanked God for the beautiful sunrise in such an

amazing place and for the retirement he was finally about to begin. Gene knew God's will and hand in all things was the reason for his recent successes, and for one big nuclear catastrophe being thwarted, and he thanked God several times in a row for things going the way they had.

"Amen," he said aloud, then he put his hat back on his head, climbed atop Dusty, and rode away from the barn out into the desert to check on his cattle, fences, and a few waterers in the big pastures.

The sun's direct rays made it overtop of the mountains to the east and reached Dusty and Gene before he had ridden a mile. The desert world around him flooded with bright orange light and nearly overwhelmed his senses. Gene reflected on the days he had spent with his grandfather when he was young and how this moment reminded him of many such days back then.

Everything looked to be in order as Gene rode through his pastures: fences, numbers of cattle here and there, and waterers. He bet that Gunny had spent time each day riding those geldings and checking on things. Time melted away for Gene as Dusty and he traveled for miles, and the air quickly warmed up.

Ring, ring! The cell phone broke the landscape's spell on him.

Gene snatched the flip phone from the phone holster on his belt and flipped it open with the thumb of the same hand.

"Yeah," he said.

"Well, hero, is that all you've got to say?"

"Naw, Jeb—what I want to say is, 'See what happens when you don't answer your phone when I call, like back at JFK the other morning?' You get me into some sticky wickets, brother!"

"How about, 'Gee, Jeb, thanks for getting me out of jail and making the whole stealing an antique fighter plane, ignoring about 50 federal laws, having a dogfight right over downtown Manhattan, deliberately crashing into another plane over said city center, and landing a plane in the middle of West Street go away?'

That would work."

"Bull snot!" Gene replied.

There was a long pause.

"That's it?" Jeb asked. "Bull snot? What does that mean, anyway?"

"That means you pulled me out of my first week of retirement—literally from the middle of my first branding on my very own ranch—and get me mixed up in tracking some global terrorist conspiracy. I can't believe I answered the phone just now, come to think of it! 'Bull snot' doesn't even begin to cover it, Jeb. Speaking of covering it, I do get overtime for all that work, right?"

"Overtime?" Jeb said in an astonished voice. "You're retired. You're not getting paid at all, you old coot."

"What?" Gene feigned amazement and smiled. "Oh that's right; I forgot. I'm actually a civilian contractor now. I'm in a considerably higher pay bracket. I'm sending you my bill—lots of zeros in front of the decimal place."

"Yeah, all zeros!" Jeb ribbed back at him. "But in all seriousness, Gene, two things. First, that one-time pad you came up with...it hasn't helped with any of the other numbers station messages, so you got incredibly lucky it deciphered the one it did, my friend! But, that business you told me about a bunch of duplicate Soviet one-time pads from the 40s. That checked out and we were able to decipher one of the other messages with that info...our agents are seeing where that leads to now. Second, take a ride down to the airpark and see Conrad. There is a little something for you there."

"Oh no," Gene replied. "I'm not falling for that one again! I'm staying put on the ranch this time."

"No, no...you're going to like this one. Trust me. And don't tell me you didn't love saving New York City from nuclear devastation. So get your little dogies on down there."

"Jeb, I'm hanging up now."

"Git along little...."

Click. Gene slapped the phone shut on Jeb and chuckled. Then curiosity got the better of him and he turned Dusty back in the direction of the airpark and they set out at a brisk walk.

***

Dusty trotted in the sand off to the side of the gravel road that led from the Lazy G to the airpark. As they approached Conrad's place Gene could see the skeleton of the Sopwith Pup parked outside the hanger in the road.

"That's odd," Gene thought. "Why would Conrad have the Pup outside the hanger if he's still working on it?"

Dusty and Gene stopped in front of Conrad's hanger and the old airman stepped out of the man-sized door in the front corner of the metal building.

"Heya, old man!" Gene said as he slid down out of the saddle.

"Old? Now I'm gunna let you in a on a secret...you actually look about ten years older than when I saw you about a week ago," Conrad said, squinting at his neighbor in the sunlight. "Retirement must be kind of hard on you."

"Retirement?" Gene shot back at him. "Yeah, right! Hey, what's the Pup doing outside?"

"Oh, just cleaning up the hanger...you know," Conrad said, with a big grin on his face. "Oh, by the way, a guy came by and left you a little something. It's just inside the hanger here—hold on; I'll get it for you."

"Okay," Gene said, thinking Conrad was acting a little fishy as the old airman turned on his heel and in his oily cover-alls sort of skipped back through the hanger door.

Grrrrrrr...an electric motor began to hum and the big hanger door began to rise slowly. Gene could see the darkness of the interior of the hanger become exposed through the opening at the bottom. It continued to rise and when it got to a few feet high,

Gene could see the landing gear of some sizable plane inside.

Grrrrrrr...the door continued to rise. When the sun fully illuminated what was inside the hanger, Gene's jaw dropped and he stood there in utter amazement.

"Well?" Conrad said, reemerging from the hanger and smiling from ear to ear at his stupefied friend. "A guy flew it in yesterday. Said it was a gift for you for saving Manhattan and stopping World War III, if you ever got out of jail, that is. He said he had his mechanics work around the clock for a couple of days to get it right for you—back into mint condition. Oh, yeah, and he said he expected to see it at some air shows during the year, and he highly suggested that you get the original .50 cals installed back in it and armed—which, you know, I could do for you, by the way...."

Gene just stood there holding Dusty's reins, his jaw dropped, and utterly speechless. The P-51 Mustang was shining vibrantly in the light that poured into the hanger, and there on the nose was a pin-up girl with the words, "Hard To Get."

"Okay, I'll take that as a maybe on the .50 cals...." Conrad said.

Yip, yip!

"Oh, and another thing," Conrad continued, while enjoying watching the bewildered look on Gene's face. "A little air transport plane landed here yesterday. Weird, right? I mean, we've never had an air transport plane just show up here before. I tell you, Gene, having you in the neighborhood is turning out to be a real gas! Who knew you were so popular? So this plane lands and I go out to see what it's about, and the guy says he's been hired special to deliver you a package pronto, and could I help with directions to your ranch. I explained that you were in prison for who knew how long, but that I could sign for it and would keep it here safe until you made parole or whatever and got out of the clink."

Yip!

"Over here behind the Mustang you have a big crate," Conrad continued, stepping into the hanger. "So there's a Sopwith Pup outside, a Quarter Horse outside, a Mustang inside, and look... another pup inside, too. It's a real zoo around here!"

Conrad gave a hearty laugh at his own musings. Gene's gaze was hard pressed to be distracted from the amazing Mustang he had just been gifted, but the furry little fellow who came scampering out of the hanger right up to Gene and tried to climb up his left leg was able to get his full attention.

"What's this, Conrad?"

"Looks like a Boarder Collie puppy to me," Conrad replied.

"Yes, I realize that!" Gene said, laughing. "I mean, what the heck...where did he come from?"

"Well, all I can tell you is that he came from that air travel dog crate over there, and this letter was handed off with him."

Gene picked up the puppy and looked into two eyes that revealed intensity and intelligence, and were an unusual amber color.

"Oh, you rascal," Gene said, grinning at the little furry ball. "You are something, aren't you? Let's see where you came from."

Gene put the puppy down and took the letter from Conrad and opened it. On fine stationary that Gene instantly recognized from many decades earlier with Hôtel Le Bristol Paris written in fancy script at the top:

"Can't make it to the ranch now, darling. It was wonderful seeing you. Here's a little something to remember me by...."

"Aglaya," Gene said aloud.

"What's that?" Conrad asked him.

"Oh, nothing."

"Well, who's it from?"

"Just an old..." Gene thought for a moment with a distant look in his eyes, "enemy."

"That's a mighty fine present!" Conrad replied. "Y'all must have buried the hatchet."

"We did, Conrad. That we certainly did."

The End.

www.ingramcontent.com/pod-product-compliance
Lightning Source LLC
Chambersburg PA
CBHW050520260626
47157CB00004B/1401